STAR WARS HUNTERS™

BATTLE FOR THE ARENA

Written by

MARK OSHIRO

Illustrated by

ANDIE TONG

BASED ON THE GAME BY
ZYNGA AND LUCASFILM GAMES

LUCASFILM
PRESS

LOS ANGELES · NEW YORK

Printed in the United States of America

First Edition, November 2022

1 3 5 7 9 10 8 6 4 2

Library of Congress Control Number on file

FAC-038091-22259

ISBN 978-1-368-07603-6

Visit the official *Star Wars* website at: www.starwars.com.

HE HAD FINALLY FOUND HER.

From a freighter on Utapau to a transport ship on Bothawui, he had made his way back to Corellia. Back to Coronet City. Back to the place where she'd ruined everything.

And where no one had heard of her since.

He'd scoured the Core Worlds. The Colonies. The Inner Rim.

Until he'd heard stories of a strange frontwoman for a band who played the cantinas on Nar Shaddaa. One day she had just disappeared. And then . . . confirmation. He had found her on a planet that few had visited before a certain legendary Hutt collector made it her new base of operations.

Vespaara . . .

He rebuilt his crew.

He rebuilt his family.

He rebuilt himself.

And now, as he watched her in the arena for the first time, he was ready to set his plan in motion.

Let the games begin.

1

AS RIEVE BLASTED Daq Dragus's door from the tracks, she remembered that it was the second time she'd done this.

The first time seemed like a lifetime before. She had rushed there from Nar Shaddaa after seeing the ad on the holonet while she was in the transport station:

> ### ARE YOU LOOKING FOR SOMETHING NEW?
> ### DO YOU HAVE A RARE TALENT?
> ### CAN YOU COMPETE FOR GLORY?

There was an image in the background: a Rodian and a Wookiee in combat. Then it changed to a bounty hunter and a stormtrooper firing blasters at each other.

Rieve found the idea of becoming a professional Hunter in Balada the Hutt's arena appealing, but more important, the timing was perfect. Rieve could leave behind her life cleanly. It would be a *choice*, rather than something she'd been forced into, as she had in the past.

Plus, getting to perform for others but in a completely new way? It was exciting. It was a little scary. And it gave her something to channel her energy into. She hopped on the next transport to Vespaara, and she vowed to make an impression.

So Rieve decided to use the Force to break open Daq Dragus's door.

The thing had flown off its tracks and clattered to the side, and Dragus had leapt up from his desk. He wore a dark blue suit with a white undershirt and an orange neck scarf, and she would come to understand that Dragus *always* dressed like he was about to put on a show. "Just who do you think—"

"I'm here to be your next H

got any openings?"

He stared at her, his mouth

destroy my door?"

Rieve looked down at it beside h

she said.

Dragus, still a bit wary of her, step

you do that? Grappling hook?"

He examined her and saw that all she h

bag in one hand.

"Clearly, you didn't use equipment to aid

"So . . . something else."

"The Force."

Dragus actually laughed at her. "The Force?

"Yep."

"Like . . . *the* Force."

"Does it go by another name?"

"The thing those mythological Jedi supposedly u

At that, Rieve stepped closer. "You'd do good to re

"Never have been, never will."

r a moment, still as Vintian rock

ragus.

. "I suppose."

aren't afraid of upsetting me."

Not in this context."

away from her and back to his desk. "I

e said. "Balada the Hutt. She's the one who

. I usually seek out Hunters, but she has final

ryone. This is *her* arena, and I work for Balada,

way around. So she's the one to impress."

suggesting I *can't* impress her?"

Dragus laughed *really* hard. "Oh, you're a feisty

that." He rubbed his chin. "Fine. You're in."

e that, she had earned a chance to become a Hunter.

Balada's later protests—Dragus had never offered

someone Balada had not also met—Rieve joined a

handful of recruits, fighters, warriors, and malcontents from all over the galaxy, each of them aiming for one of the coveted Hunter roles. It had kick-started nearly a month of training and tests. Every day, she got up, made her way to the arena facility, and ran through countless drills, technique classes, and character-building exercises. That last one had gotten her a little freaked out.

"Why do I have to build my 'character,' Dragus?" she had asked him after her first week of training. "Can't I just *fight*?"

"Rieve, Rieve, Rieve," he said, circling her on the training grounds. They stood in between two rows of automated bot fighters, programmed to burst up at random to help hone reaction time. "You will not just be a fighter in an arena. You will be a *Hunter*."

"Who am I hunting?" Her eyes went wide with mischief. "Do I get to eat it afterward?"

"Not that kind of hunting, Rieve," he said, rolling his eyes. "We're building something special here, and I know you've seen matches in the arena."

"Sure. Seems like a lot of beating up or getting beat up. Which is just my style."

"It's not just that. Remember, I am a showman." He spread his arms wide. "Being a Hunter is more than just pummeling someone else. You will embody an entire persona when you're out in that arena. Take Sentinel. His persona is a stormtrooper who championed the Empire until it no longer suited him, and now he is using his skills for battle. People come to watch him because he's so very easy to hate. Which you'll understand if you make a roster and become a Hunter."

"Okay," said Rieve. "But is everyone like that?"

"No, not at all," explained Dragus. "Half the fun is coming up with all the personalities and traits you'll have for your persona in the arena. Take Utooni, the Jawa twins. They *really* love playing up their fighting style to be mischievous and deceiving. You get the idea?"

"I guess," she said, and she brushed the long strip of white hair down the middle of her head to one side. "But if I get this and I become a Hunter . . . who will I be?"

"You actually gave me the idea back when you so rudely entered my office."

"I like where this is going," she said.

"I want you to be a Sith Lord."

She'd initially hated the idea because . . . well, because she wasn't a Sith Lord. She had been a courier on Corellia, and she'd played in a band on Nar Shaddaa. Nothing to do with the Force. She was merely sensitive to it. It gave her some abilities—if you could call the outbursts of energy she was prone to abilities—but that was it.

But as she practiced and trained more, leaning into her ferocity and anger, she found the role of an infamous Sith Lord incredibly entertaining. She came up with a voice. A fighting style. She even helped with potential designs for a costume.

None of which she'd had the chance to use in the arena yet, at least not for real.

Now, as she stood before Dragus in his office once again, she wasn't sure she was *ever* going to be able to. She held her datapad in one hand, and this time, Dragus wasn't alone; his business partner, Balada the Hutt, loomed on the other side of his office. It worried Rieve that Balada was there. She spent most of her time in the giant ship that floated over the arena, except when she was off scouring the galaxy for a possible new weapon, trinket, or Hunter who could be added to her collection.

Well, Rieve would make this moment work for her.

"You know, we typically knock around here," Dragus said coolly.

"*Me keepuna wermo,*" Balada muttered, and while Rieve's understanding of Huttese was limited to her time on Nar Shaddaa, she got the gist:

I'm gonna shoot this fool.

Rieve ignored her. She slammed the datapad on Dragus's desk, right next to the brown boots he had propped up on it.

"Where am I?" she said.

Dragus smiled but did not look down at the datapad. "You're on Vespaara."

She glared at him. Oh, so he was in one of *those* moods. It had worked in her favor the day she had first burst into his office, but now? She needed him to take her seriously! She had traveled so far to get there; there was nowhere else she could go. Certainly not back to Coronet City.

Even if she would be welcomed there again after—

Never mind.

"Cheekta rocka rocka."

Okay, she had no idea what *that* meant.

"Well, *I* don't think Rieve's got anything wrong with her brain," said Dragus, but then he twirled around in his chair to face her. "Do you?"

"You didn't answer my question." She tapped the datapad with her finger. "Where am I? I looked over that training schedule three times. I don't see my name on it anywhere."

"I realize that." Dragus stood up and walked around his desk to a large monitor with a shiny screen mounted on the wall opposite. When he touched it, an overhead image of the arena sprang to life. She could see each of the battlefields that made up the complex, linked with one another by underground tunnels and aboveground paths.

There was Frontline on Hoth. The Ewok Village on the

Forest Moon of Endor. Aftermath, which managed to start as Hoth on one end and become Endor on the other. They'd even built what she was told was a pretty accurate replication of an outpost on Tatooine. Not that Rieve had ever heard of the place, let alone been there.

Dragus twisted a knob to zoom in on a flashing red light on the Frontline map. "We've got a malfunctioning platform here, so I'm going to head down to make sure it's fixed," he said, speaking directly to Balada.

Rieve stepped in front of him. "I asked you a question."

But Dragus was still staring at Balada. "See? I told you she had the right attitude."

Balada grunted but said nothing. She was taller than most Hutts Rieve had met over the years, and she also dressed far more fashionably. That day she wore a sleek black cloak that ran down her large body to cover most of her muscular tail.

"Do you think you have the skill, though?" Dragus continued, staring at the map.

"You know I do," Rieve shot back. "Or you wouldn't have had me train with the other potential Hunters."

"I recall letting you train because you used the Force to fling the door across my office, remember? Do you know when I last saw a person use the Force? That would be *never*."

She smiled at that. "Fair enough. I might seem new and exciting to you, but I assure you I've got the skill you need."

This time, he glanced at her and grinned. "You could be good for business," he said. "Maybe I should give you a second chance."

"A second one? When did I lose the *first* one?"

When Dragus didn't answer, she picked up her datapad and pressed a button to bring up a new image. "I saw this, by the way." She held out the datapad, and a moving advertisement flashed across it. It was definitely a recording of a training session Rieve had had a few days before. "'Come see a real-life Sith Lord!'" she read. "So you're advertising me as a Hunter but not letting me fight?"

"Who said I am—"

"I've been training for nearly a month," she continued. "Early morning drills, character workshops, tours of the arena, verbal and digital exams to measure my knowledge of arena policies and rules, and after all this, you just . . . drop me? Did I mess up at some point? Why didn't you tell me?"

Balada the Hutt broke into laughter, the booming sound filling Dragus's office.

"Why does she think this is funny?" said Rieve. "Because *I* don't think this is funny."

"It's because you're not in on the joke, kid," said Dragus.

"What joke?"

"The one where you're not on the training schedule because you're an official Hunter now."

She was speechless as heat rushed to her cheeks. It didn't help that Balada roared even louder with laughter. *"Wermo grandio!"* she said, coughing the words out between her laughs.

Rieve had heard that term before, and truthfully, she kind of *did* feel like a fool.

"You're serious," she said once Balada calmed down. "An actual Hunter?"

"Actual," said Dragus.

A smile spread across her face. "And this isn't a joke?"

He chuckled. "No, Rieve, it's not. You have done a phenomenal job in training the last month." She made to say something, but Dragus put up a hand to stop her. "I know it might be a little early. We are still building your character, for example, and no one has figured out what special signature move a Sith Lord might have. Plus, you haven't had a whole lot of time to work on team-building exercises, but Balada and I . . . we think you're ready."

Rieve felt a burst of excitement race down her spine. "Thank you," she said, her voice as even as she could make it.

"No need to thank anyone," said Dragus. "If you're serious, I'll have the forms and contracts sent to your datapad."

"I'm very serious," she said. "The most serious person you will ever meet."

"And you know you can't fight in any other arena. This is your only competitive venture."

"Of course."

"Perfect," he said. "All that's left is for you to do a good job tonight."

She froze. "Wait. What?"

He raised an eyebrow. "Tonight. Your first battle. Welcome to being a Hunter."

A new emotion flared in Rieve, and this one . . . this one was a little more dangerous. If things got to be too overwhelming, there was a chance she wouldn't be able to keep herself under control.

And she couldn't risk that.

So she stood as straight as she could. "I won't disappoint you," she said.

"Hagwa," Balada crooned, then brushed past the two of them and out of Dragus's office.

"What did she say?" asked Rieve.

" 'Don't,' " said Dragus.

"Don't what?"

He smiled again, but it didn't reach the rest of his face.

"Don't disappoint us."

He walked over to the doorway of his office, gesturing for Rieve to leave.

She gulped her fear down. Tonight. She could do that.

She left Dragus's office, still a little unsure of what she was getting herself into.

2

R *IEVE KNEW SHE'D HAVE TO* find a better way to keep track of time. She was nearly late, and it didn't help that Vespaara had one of the strangest skies she'd ever seen. There, it was always twilight, that hour just before the sun disappeared below the horizon. It was pretty to look at—especially that constantly changing aurora in the sky—but it meant any given moment of the day felt exactly like every other one.

It was an adjustment for sure. But she showed her scandocs to one of the security droids at the back entrance to the arena complex, she was waved in, and then . . . she ran.

Past trainers and medical droids.

Past Charr, the Trandoshan, and Skora, the Rodian, who were geared up and clearly on their way to a battle in the arena with that night's second roster.

Past a slow-moving tech team, who took up the entire tunnel.

She didn't feel all that bad for using the Force to slightly nudge them to the side.

With just a few seconds to spare, she burst into the backstage area.

Located underneath the arena, backstage was humming with activity. She hadn't been down there much, and every time she had? The place was too overwhelming for her. She thought it looked like a hive of Corellian gluttonbugs: people scurried about from station to station, somehow not colliding with one another. There was an odd hum that hung over everything, an eerie combination of the machinery that kept the arena running and the drone of conversation among the techs, droids, and med staff.

Rieve's eyes skimmed over the empty bacta tanks and landed on the long stretch of prep pods that was her destination. Much of the second roster were prepping for their matches, which were set to start shortly. There was an enormous screen in the center of the room, and techs sat on all sides of it, monitoring every aspect of the arena: Which battlefield was active. Which special effects were used. What the status of any given Hunter on the field was. There were overhead camera feeds from the vantage point of Balada the Hutt's ship, which floated over the arena, as well as the camera droids that captured footage for the holonet feed.

If she stood there long enough, all the images and sounds would make her brain feel like it was going to short-circuit, so she made straight for her prep pod. She was nearly there when she was stopped.

By J-3DI.

"Good evening, new recruit," he said. "Daq Dragus said that I was to help get you situated before our first match together!"

J-3DI didn't tower over Rieve, but he was still the tallest droid she'd ever seen. He had a small, disklike head with glowing eyes over a body built to look impressive and agile.

He was already styled out as a Jedi warrior, complete with a sweeping brown robe.

Rieve didn't like J-3DI that much.

She thought he meant well, as well as someone pro-grammed to be a knowledgeable Jedi could mean. Sometimes, though, he was . . . a lot. He had a seemingly endless database of information that he *loved* to share whenever he thought it was appropriate to do so. Which turned out to be all the time! In the few weeks since he'd appeared, he'd had a tendency to drone on and on to Rieve about elements of the Force or Jedi lore, despite the fact that she was *actually* Force-sensitive. He was just a droid.

Some days, she didn't want to admit that she was also a little bitter. She'd gradually met some of the other Hunters who fought in the arena, but they were still strangers to her. All of them, however, seemed really friendly with J-3DI. It wasn't a competition, of course, but . . . maybe it was. Just a bit.

As J-3DI whisked her through the backstage area, droning on and on about the support team that surrounded them, she realized that his existence was probably a sign that Dragus was *always* going to keep her as part of the team. Why build a Jedi Knight to compete against a Sith Lord if you weren't going to hire the person trying out for the Sith Lord persona in the first place?

It didn't matter anymore, though. All she had to do was prove herself.

"Rieve?"

She snapped out of her thoughts and looked at J-3DI. "What?"

"I asked if you're familiar with our exact match styles," he said.

Rieve was watching as a set of techs rushed off into a tunnel that led to the Ewok Village battlefield. She nodded her head absently at J-3DI.

"Well, I think a refresher could help," he continued.

"Sure," she said, her attention wandering. He was going to start telling her things she already knew, wasn't he?

"So, there are generally two types of matches you'll be competing in on any given day," said J-3DI.

Yep, she thought. *We went over this on the second day of training!*

"Though I've heard talk of there being a third match style."

That got her attention. "A third? But I've only trained on Control and Escort."

"I wouldn't worry," he said. "Word is that Dragus is thinking of adding a shortened version of Huttball in the Gauntlet battlefield."

Huttball? Oh, Rieve *liked* Huttball. There was a larger arena nearby devoted solely to the sport, and Hunters were known to gather for scrimmage matches after-hours with some of the professional Huttballers. The sport was exceptionally brutal at times, and when Rieve needed a release after a frustrating day, she loved throwing her weight around playing Huttball.

"But we'll cross that bridge when we get to it," said J-3DI.

Rieve looked at him, scratching her head. "What bridge? Are we fighting on a bridge?"

"No," said J-3DI. "There are platforms and some aerial passageways in the Ewok Village——"

"Jay-Three, I'm joking."

He paused and examined her with his ocular processers,

one blue, the other white. "Yes. Of course. A joke! I am familiar with those. My maker, Sprocket—Have you met him? He tells many jokes. Perhaps he'll update my programming with some of them."

She wanted to crack another one at his expense, but he pushed on without a break. "There is Escort, in which you have a payload to deliver to the opposite side of the battlefield. Your team must stay close to it to keep it moving. You might also compete in Control, in which your team must capture a designated point and hold it until the time expires in the match."

"I'm aware, Jay-Three. You know I went through training, right?"

"And I assume you also know that you are randomly assigned a team each day, too."

"Of course," she said, though she quietly wished that wasn't the case. She wasn't exactly thrilled by the idea of having to one day play on the same team as J-3DI.

"Have you met your trainer yet?"

"My who?"

Rieve wasn't sure it was possible, but she thought she could hear the overeager smile in J-3DI's voice. "Oh, your trainer is your most important point of contact here. They will help you get into character, treat immediate medical issues, repair weapons and gear, and in general, they exist to assist you."

"Sounds great," she said, but her attention was already wandering again. She could see the remaining Hunters preparing for that night's competition.

There was Zaina, the Rebel Scout, who sat next to her trainer as they helped her with her prosthetic legs.

Next to her were the twin Jawas who made up Utooni. Outside of the long red cloak they used in the arena, they were in . . . smaller brown cloaks. *Well, at least they're committed to the mystery,* thought Rieve. The two were arguing about something. One of them turned to Rieve and offered up a quick wave of welcome, and Rieve returned it.

Grozz, a Wookiee and former professional Huttball player, was being stretched by his trainer, a tall Dor Namethian male. Sentinel, the ex-Imperial soldier, was examining his E-Web heavy repeater. The Bounty Hunter, Imara Vex, was a dark-skinned human female, and she twisted up her hair locs so they would fit underneath her Ubese-style helmet. Whenever she wasn't planet-hopping on a bounty-hunting job, she was a formidable force in the arena. Dizzy, an Ugnaught who was utterly inseparable from his droideka, was shouting at his trainer in a rapid-fire tongue about something. Once he entered the arena, though, he became Slingshot, the chaotic fighter who stalked other Hunters with his customized droideka.

So. This was her roster. This was who she'd be fighting with or against every day in the arena. Was it fair that she didn't really know them? Maybe J-3DI had had his familiarity with the others programmed into him.

She took a deep breath as she approached her prep pod with J-3DI. All she had to do was fight well, and she'd be fine. Plus, she had the element of surprise on her side. Rieve might not know the other Hunters, but they also didn't know *anything* about her.

Rieve's prep pod was built into a large recess in the wall, lit brightly from above, and big enough for three or four people to be in it at once. For now, there was only a human male placing meds and wraps on a small shelf on the far side of the pod. He turned and stood at attention as they approached.

"Ah," said J-3DI, "your trainer is already here!"

The man—just as tall as J-3DI—held out a pale hand. He had short-cropped brown hair and a plain face. "Rothwell," he said as they shook hands. "I'll be your trainer here in the arena."

"It is actually Rothwell's first day, as well," said J-3DI, lingering near the prep pod. "He arrived here two days ago to begin preparations for—"

"Wait," said Rieve, holding up her hand to interrupt J-3DI. "Two days?"

Rothwell nodded.

"So that means . . ." Rieve shook her head. "Balada *definitely* had made the decision to offer me the Hunter role when she sent that ad out."

J-3DI appeared to be processing for a moment. "Correct," he said. "Perhaps earlier, given that I was first activated by

Sprocket a week ago so that you, a Hunter who is actually Force-sensitive, had a competitor in the arena uniquely matched to you."

She scoffed at that. "Uniquely matched," she repeated, then looked over at Rothwell. "I'm going to destroy him today."

"Unlikely," said J-3DI. "I possess the most updated operating code in the galaxy, as well as all of the current Jedi lore available."

Rieve stepped close to J-3DI. "But do you know how to fight?"

J-3DI hesitated. "We will see tonight, Rieve." Then he bowed dramatically. "May the Force be on you, young Sith Lord."

That left Rieve speechless for a moment. She had learned firsthand that Sprocket's programming of J-3DI often missed its mark. She didn't correct him, though. *Let him be wrong,* she thought. She kind of liked the subtle advantage it gave her.

Rothwell was waiting for her. "Let's get started," he said. "We got a lot to do."

She held up a finger. "Not yet," she said, and she dug into her cloak and pulled out an audiochip. "I need this to prepare to."

Rothwell took it and examined it for a moment. "Music?" he said.

She nodded.

Moments later, the first squeal of feedback echoed in the pod, followed by galloping drums and then a stampede of sound. Aggressive vocals were shouted over it all, and a smile spread over Rieve's face.

"Gonkrock?" said Rothwell.

Rieve raised her eyebrows. "You familiar with it?"

"Yeah. Had some friends on Nar Shaddaa years back. They never stopped talking about it."

She wondered what Rothwell would think if she told him that she'd fronted a gonkrock band. The style originated from groups who ran their amplifiers through GNK-series power droids, so the name just stuck. It was loud. It was fast.

And she would never share that it seemed to speak to her through the Force.

Rothwell didn't complain; he just jumped to work, helping strip Rieve of her street clothes and wrapping her in the proprietary bandage tape that Balada the Hutt mandated all organic Hunters use. Rothwell spoke only to explain that Balada had "found" the material in some distant system and discovered it was perfect to help limit potential injury.

"So what is it?" Rieve asked. "And why have I never heard of something like this before?"

Rothwell shrugged. "They don't tell me much, either."

Otherwise, Rothwell said nothing. He moved with an efficient, perfectionist speed. Once fully wrapped, Rieve stood in front of a mirror, examining how the tape almost disappeared against her skin. It made her tall, muscular form seem *more* tall and muscular.

Rothwell helped Rieve into the black-and-red outfit that clung to her skin but still stretched so she could breathe easily. He wrapped her arms and legs. He had her sit still as he applied her face paint, which would help her sink into the character of Rieve the Sith Lord. She'd kept her hair long and white, her natural color, though she had deep undercuts on either side of her head, her hair shaved down to the scalp. The makeup was simple but effective: geometric shapes on her forehead and two sharp red streaks that ran from beneath her eyes to her neck. She loved how it accented her angular features.

But it was the loud, vicious music that put her in the right frame of mind. She disappeared into herself and her thoughts. If she channeled her energy, like she was funneling her power through her anger and her rage, then she could control herself on the battlefield. The more stability she had, the better her performance. At least, that was what she had discovered in training.

Rothwell raised a hand. "Mind if I turn off the music? Just for this last part."

She nodded, and Rothwell turned off the gonkrock.

He approached and placed his pointer fingers on either side of her collar, where it nearly met at the center of her neck. "You've got two comms built into the collar of your outfit," Rothwell explained. "You can communicate with your team or with me while I'm here backstage."

He stepped away from her and tapped something on his datapad. "Can you hear me?"

It was an odd sensation; there was barely a delay between the words that came out of Rothwell's mouth and what Rieve heard. "Yeah," she said. "Loud and clear."

"Excellent. Now, only your teammates each day can hear you, and we also don't transmit it to the arena's announcers or any of the holonet feeds. So don't feel like you need to edit yourself."

"What would I need this for, though?" she asked.

"Coordinating attacks in the arena," he said. "But it also helps if you get injured or something else goes wrong."

She didn't expect she'd need to use it; she had always been able to take care of herself. "Okay," she said. "Anything else? Any other weird things built into the outfit I should know about?"

Rothwell shook his head. "Nope. They wanted to keep things as easy and simple as possible."

She liked easier. She didn't want to think about all this tech and all the rules. She just wanted to fight.

This wasn't training anymore, though. Rothwell gave Rieve a once-over, then handed her the lightsaber, the final part of her persona. Rieve had heard stories about the mythical weapon, wielded by Jedi Knights and Sith. And here was one for her to use, from Balada's personal collection. Rieve had been warned to treat it with care and reverence; Balada also made it *very* clear that it was *never* to leave the arena.

Rieve took the lightsaber from Rothwell. The metal hilt was cold at first, but as it warmed in her hand, it was as if she connected with it. It became a part of her. She activated the blade and swung it gracefully back and forth.

It was time for Rieve to make her debut.

 *IEVE STOOD AT THE END* of the long tunnel that led to the Frontline battlefield. The entire thing was styled after some legendary battle between the Rebellion and the Empire on Hoth. She'd heard stories over the years about it, but it ultimately meant nothing to her. The Empire had a different meaning in Rieve's life: they were the ones who had taken over the ports in Coronet City, forcing most of the native citizens into work that best benefited the Imperial forces. It was how Rieve had gotten started as a courier in the first place.

Yet even that felt like it was a million years before. Rieve looked over at the other three Hunters she'd been partnered with on this match: Zaina, Imara Vex, and Slingshot. Zaina nodded. "You're gonna do just fine," she said, switching her blaster to her left hand so she could clap Rieve on the shoulder.

Rieve was about to reply when a boisterous male voice blared out of the comms in her collar.

"On Team Mudhorn, we've got Utooni, Jay-Threedeeaye, Sentinel, and Grozz."

"Which means they'll be facing off against Zaina, Imara Vex, Slingshot, and newcomer Rieve on Team Gundark," finished a second voice, this one much sharper and coded female.

Rieve grabbed the right edge of her collar. "Rothwell, what *is* that? Who is speaking to me?"

The first voice continued. "Lexi, it's going to be interesting to see what dynamic Rieve will bring to the arena since we know so little about her."

"Rothwell!" Rieve hissed.

"What is it?" asked Imara Vex.

"Do you have people . . . *narrating* in your comms?" asked Rieve.

Her three teammates shook their heads.

"Sorry, sorry," said Rothwell. "I accidentally had the announcers patched into your feed."

A moment later, Rieve's comms were quiet.

"I'm guessing you never saw a holonet feed of a match," said Rothwell.

"No," said Rieve. "I'm not really big on using the holonet."

"Don't blame you," he said. "But holonet viewers really seem to like the two announcers—Boz Vega and Lexi."

Rieve grimaced at that. She hadn't heard much, but what little had made it to her comms was awkward. Were they going to talk about her the entire time? Analyze her every move?

"Head in the game," said Imara Vex, and she pointed.

In front of them, there was a holographic countdown at the entrance to Frontline that was ticking down from ten.

You can do this, Rieve told herself.

She'd trained for nearly a month. She knew what she was doing. Get to the control point first, hold it until the end of the match. That was it.

Five.

She breathed in.

Four.

Let it out.

Three.

Two.

One.

There was a sharp alarm in the tunnel, and then the four Hunters began to sprint. Rieve was impressed with how easily she could move in her outfit, given how snug it fit, and she managed to tail right behind Zaina, but something new and unexpected hit her.

The roar.

Every training session Rieve had attended had been in an empty arena. Now bright lights flickered and flashed all around her as she bounded around the first corner with Zaina and onto a platform. The crowd was going absolutely *wild*, the sound so immense that Rieve couldn't find anything to focus on. So she did her best to keep her eyes on Zaina, who sprinted in a quick burst to make it into the control point before the Mudhorns. The point turned blue, signifying a Gundark occupation.

And then it was *chaos*.

Blaster fire ripped past Rieve, and she dodged it with a quick spin. She held her lightsaber in front of her and instinctively deflected another shot from Sentinel, the Stormtrooper, who loomed over her on a higher platform.

An image appeared in her head that sent a shiver down her spine:

A squadron of stormtroopers. A man in a cloak. A gathering of shadows.

Rieve told herself that this was only a game. Sentinel was playing a part, just like she was.

So she leaned into her persona, snarling in rage as she spotted J-3DI rapidly approaching. "I can smell you, Jedi!" she called out. "A mix of stale oil and singed circuits!"

Rieve raised her lightsaber up, then swung it down, connecting with J-3DI's.

"The Force expects setbacks," said J-3DI, blocking her attack. "Have at me, dark one!"

Oh, this is too fun, Rieve thought, and she released a fury of attacks, pushing J-3DI out of the control point.

He beckoned to her. "There is no chaos," he taunted. "The Force is all there is."

She laughed at that one. *What* does *that mean?* she thought. *Is he just sputtering nonsense?*

"Why do you hesitate, Rieve?" J-3DI pointed his lightsaber at her. "Afraid of a Jedi Knight?"

Well, *that* irritated her. She felt another surge of energy, and she chased after J-3DI.

"Rieve, what are you doing?" someone said in her comms.

It took a second, but she realized it was Zaina.

"I'm taking out the competition!" she said.

"We need you back at the control point!" Zaina yelled, her voice pitching higher. "We have—"

Zaina's feed cut off, and Rieve spun to look behind her. Had Zaina been taken out?

She sensed someone behind her and spun again just in time

to parry a set of blows from J-3DI. She kicked out and he wobbled off balance for a moment.

"Rieve, get back here!" Imara Vex's voice sounded frustrated in the comms. "I swear, you're worse than some of the bounties I chase!"

But Rieve had a focus. She and J-3DI went toe to toe, and for a moment she was completely in the zone. The Force coursed through her body, and she thought about using it, but . . . no. No, she didn't need it right then. Her skills as a fighter were good enough.

Then Slingshot ripped her out of her concentration. "Rieve, where are you?" he said. "Grozz just took out Imara Vex with his boulder attack! I'm at the control point by myself!"

That just pushed her harder as she swung on J-3DI, who could only defend himself at this point. He backed up into one of the covered passages in the battlefield, his blue lightsaber illuminating his face. His round eyes focused on her, but there was no emotion there. Were her attacks affecting him? She couldn't even tell. So Rieve swung, and she hit his lightsaber *hard*, so hard that he actually slid back a few meters.

"You have my attention, Sith," he said in a low voice.

It frustrated her. She should have taken him out already! Her offensive attacks had kept him on the defensive the whole time!

So she pushed him back, farther into the covered part of Frontline, and he blocked every one of her swings.

She felt her anger build in her.

She hit harder. Harder. Harder.

"Rieve!"

Slingshot again. Could she turn the comms off? They just distracted her!

"Rieve, they've got—"

Silence.

She went in for one more attack.

And that was when the gong that announced the end of the match rang out.

"Winner: Team Mudhorn," intoned a monotonous voice through the comms.

Rieve lowered her lightsaber and stared at J-3DI.

"Good match," said J-3DI in that cheery voice of his. "You are a formidable fighter! May the Forces be around you!"

Then he scuttled to the team exits, leaving Rieve bewildered and disappointed.

HE WATCHED HER.

With each swipe of her lightsaber, she seemed all the more ferocious. It didn't matter that her team had lost; he could see her potential. Her violence. Her power.

This was her.

This was the girl who had ruined his life. Who had destroyed his family.

What was she doing there, fighting in an arena? Wasn't this beneath her? When would she show her true self to those around her?

He decided to wait. Soon enough, she'd reveal what she was hiding, and then . . .

Then he would strike.

R *IEVE STOMPED THROUGH* the player exit and into the tunnels below the arena.

"Hey, don't worry," said Zaina, patting her on the back. "It's one match. I'm pretty sure each of us has been responsible for losing a match at least once."

"Exactly," said Dizzy as he rolled alongside them in his droideka. "During one of my early fights, I . . ." Dizzy sighed. "I actually ran over Sentinel. While I was on his team."

"And it was *exceptionally* funny," added Zaina.

"You're biased," said Imara Vex. "You'd run over Sentinel yourself if *you* had the chance."

"That's irrelevant," said Zaina, laughing. "We're trying to boost Rieve's self-esteem."

But Rieve wasn't even listening. Rage flowed through her body. How could she have let J-3DI taunt her like that? She had allowed her irritation with him to consume her, so much so that he was *all* she could focus on.

Rieve had just made it to her prep pod when Dragus slid up to her. He had on a glimmering purple suit. "Good match," he said, patting her arm.

She groaned. "Hardly. Is it a good match if I lost?"

"There's more to this than winning or losing," he said.

"I'm not so sure," she said, holding out her lightsaber to Rothwell, who took it to clean it. "Easy for you to say."

"I've lost my fair share, remember?"

Ah, right. Dragus used to be a fighter himself. Went by the name Durasteel. She wondered what kind of style he had.

Rieve didn't ask, though. She removed her decorative armbands and plopped them down on a small table. "I thought I had Jay-Three," she said.

"You almost did!"

"So why do you make it sound like a bad thing?"

"That isn't what these battles are for," Dragus explained. "Look, you've got an Escort battle coming up next. Try to think about it differently. Guarding the payload *with* your team all the way to the finish line takes a different type of focus and strategy. It matters just as much how you work *with* your team as it does when you work *for* them."

"Look, if you're going to lecture me with any of that hokey Jedi nonsense, save your breath. I'm supposed to be a Sith Lord, right? Wouldn't Sith Lords be selfish anyway?"

"Rieve, no one on this planet has probably ever *seen* a Jedi or a Sith," said Dragus. "Sure, we heard all the stories about the war, but do you really think I know anything about Jedi or the Force?"

She sighed. "Okay. Good point. What should I do?"

"You have a story to tell," he said. "When you're in the arena, sure, people will see a Sith Lord and make their own assumptions. But how can you be that *and* position your team for victory?"

"I guess I have to make this up as I go," she said. "I don't know a whole lot about Jedi, the Sith, or the Force, either."

"Well, that's what Jay-Three is for. You should be friends with him."

"No, absolutely not," she said, turning away from Dragus.

"At least your dislike of him is entertaining," he said. "And we are absolutely here to entertain others. Just . . . try not to treat this battle like it's *only* between you and Jay-Three."

Dragus left, and Rieve took a seat in her prep pod, letting Rothwell analyze her body for any infections, tears, or other injuries that would need to be treated. He had stayed quiet during her entire conversation with Dragus, and she appreciated that. He began to press his thumbs into a surprisingly sore spot on her thigh.

"Try not to tense up," he said softly, and she let herself sink deeper into the chair as she tried to relax. Rothwell dug harder into the tender muscle, but Rieve didn't flinch.

"Perfect," he said. "You know, for what it's worth? I thought you fought well."

"Right," she said. "You saw everything."

"Of course. It's easier to keep track of your movements that way. Then, when it comes time to help you, I have all the information I need so you don't have to explain everything over the comms."

"Oh. Well . . . thanks." She relaxed further.

"No problem. Any other soreness or pain I should know about?"

She shook her head.

"Then let's get you wrapped up, stretched, and you can be on your way."

They went through all the prep routines in silence, except for Rothwell's occasional command, each of them curt but still polite. She liked him. There was no nonsense to him. He was there to do his job and do it well.

And he liked her fighting. That was a plus.

Rieve thought of blaring more gonkrock during her stretches, but her thoughts were already too loud. Too sharp around the edges. She knew she was a skilled fighter, and it *was* true that despite all J-3DI's programming, she'd kept him off her the entire battle. But this idea of teamwork . . . it frustrated her. What was she supposed to do? Ignore her abilities?

Not fight back? Why couldn't the rest of her team have picked up the slack? If they hadn't been taken out, it wouldn't have mattered that she was busy trying to eliminate the droid.

Fine. She would take Dragus's advice, if only to prove to him that she could stick with the payload.

 **HE DID NOT STICK WITH** the payload.

Rieve was in her prep pod after the match, and she'd dismissed Rothwell, telling him that she needed a moment alone. She was watching a playback of the battle on her datapad.

"This newcomer," said the announcer Boz Vega, incredulous, "do you think she knows that the purpose of this match style is literally spelled out in the name?"

"One wonders," said his counterpart, L-X1. "You're supposed to stay with the payload to keep it moving across the battlefield, and yet . . ."

"And yet, Lexi! Our newest Hunter, a fierce Sith Lord, just can't seem to follow—"

Rieve switched it off. She couldn't bear to watch herself make the *exact* same mistake again. J-3DI had started goading her away from the payload, only this time he had Sentinel alongside him. They teamed up, and she fell for it, completely and utterly.

The words of her teammates yelled over the comms replayed in her mind.

Zaina, trying to urge her to stay on target: "Let's get on it!"

Slingshot, irritation in his voice as the timer ran down and down: "We gotta beat the clock!"

Imara Vex growled over the comms at the last second: "I hate to lose!"

They were kind to her afterward. They made comments about how it was her first day and she had lots to learn. They told her they were looking forward to being on her team again.

But that voice in Rieve's head—the one she had started hearing as a teenager, right before everything changed and she had to run—was always the loudest. And it was over-whelming now.

It told her that she was never going to figure this out.

It told her that she was always going to lose.

It told her that her fellow Hunters were happier before she joined the team.

It told her that she would never fit in.

When that voice was the loudest . . . well, Rieve knew exactly what would happen.

And it would be explosive.

She left the arena without a word to anyone. There were more matches scheduled for the next day, and she'd have another chance to lose herself in the fight, but right then, she needed a release for what was building up inside her.

She exited the arena into the eternal twilight of Vespaara, briefly glancing up at Balada's *Hypernova*-class control ship, which floated overhead. The aurora beyond it swirled in reds and purples.

There was so much sky there. Rieve's true home, Coronet City on Corellia, was so *different*. Unless you were out on the water or in the industrial district, the sky was more like an idea than a reality. She was used to tall buildings of glass and metal that stretched up above her, mag-lev train lines snaking between them.

Vespaara was too new for any of that. The story went that Balada the Hutt found it by accident while on a scouting journey, seeking out the next oddity to add to her collection. The eternal twilight and the shifting aurora *were* stunning. But this planet in the Outer Rim also had a side that forever tilted away from the closest star, meaning it was at just the right temperature to be habitable. In the past year, an entire boomtown had sprung up around the arena Balada had had constructed.

Rieve lived in the small but bustling Employee District, named so because it was where all the athletes, racers, Hunters, and supporting staff were housed. It was made up of homes, small restaurants able to offer up food quickly, and rowdy cantinas. Rieve's place was tiny, tucked behind a cantina the Huttballers frequented. She hadn't brought a whole lot with her when she hopped on a transport from Coronet City to Nar Shaddaa, then to Vespaara, so the size didn't bother her.

Over the past month, she'd kept to herself, too. Each

group in the district tended to stick with their own for the most part. The podracers thought the Huttball players were "uncivilized," and the Huttball players thought the podracers' sport was too safe. However, Hunters and Huttballers usually got along, and there was an open invitation to any Hunter who wanted in on a pickup game.

And right now, she needed a release.

So she didn't go home. She drifted past the roar of the podracing track and headed straight for the Huttball facility, the only competitive entertainment on Vespaara that was entirely indoors. They had their own arena, and while it wasn't as big as Balada's, it was still impressive. The building towered over the surrounding neighborhood, and she could see some patrons leaving it. The night's matches were already over, so she hoped to find one of the infamous pickup scrimmage matches.

Rieve needed to run. To kick and shove and feel her own strength as she barreled into another player. Huttball had a much more brutal reputation than the Hunters' arena.

It was perfect.

Rieve flashed her scandocs at the door, since there was an unspoken policy that Hunters and Huttballers could access each other's arenas. She could already hear the echoes of a scrimmage game in play. She made her way into the largely empty arena. There were a few folks in the stands watching the match unfold on the field.

Rieve stood at the edge of the stands and hoped to find an opening in one of the teams so she could squeeze in. She was surprised when a furry hand clamped down on her shoulder. She spun, ready for a possible confrontation, but relaxed at the sight of Grozz.

He cooed at her in Shyriiwook.

She tilted her head and frowned. She'd never learned the language.

Grozz threw his head back and made a sound like a laugh. It kind of seemed like it was directed at her, but she wasn't sure. Irritation flared, but then Grozz pointed at her. Then himself. Then he made both his hands into fists and bashed them together while saying a word over and over.

Rieve realized she didn't need to know what the word was because she understood. He was inviting her to play!

She nodded furiously. "Yes, yes," she said. "I would *love* to."

Not long after that, Grozz flagged down the unofficial referee, a Cerean, who trotted over. Grozz bellowed something at them, and they turned to Rieve. "A new Hunter, eh?" they said to her with an incline of their tall, pointed head. "You're always welcome here for a game."

"Thanks," she said, a little set back by the kindness they showed. "Got room for me in an upcoming round?"

"We got room for *both* of you, if you like." They waved Grozz and Rieve into the arena, and she hopped over the separating wall, landing gracefully on the arena floor. There was a brief huddle with the existing players, who then turned to Rieve and Grozz with something like a hungry joy on their faces, as if to say, *Excellent, fresh meat!*

Oh, this was going to be *good*.

Moments later, the game began. It was easy to pick up on in theory: Two teams tried to toss the Huttball into the opposing team's goal. But then there were the raised platforms. Oh, and the fire traps. *And* the shock pylons. The entire place was alive in one way or another, and if you didn't pay attention . . . well, you went down.

Rieve lined up alongside Grozz on their side of the arena. She waited for the call to play.

She *sprinted*.

Energy thrummed through her body. There, she could let loose without a massive crowd watching, something that no training could have prepared Rieve for. She thought about blaming her poor performance in the match that day on not being used to having a live audience screaming at her, but even she knew that would have been a pathetic excuse. That wasn't why her team lost.

Still, as she bounded for the Huttball, she was thankful for how easy it was for her to focus there. The Force came alive inside her. She could sense the other team in a way she couldn't earlier that day in the Hunters' arena because now she could *concentrate*.

She grabbed the Huttball.

And the chase was on.

She dodged two humans, then a female Iakaru, who fell to the floor when Rieve spun around her. She could sense someone racing to tackle her, but it didn't matter. The goal was in sight.

She heaved the ball toward it, and it was an effortless score.

Her teammates cheered, and Grozz bumped his chest against her arm, calling out victoriously. She nearly went flying across the arena floor; Rieve thought that maybe Grozz had forgotten he was a Wookiee and she was a human.

Rieve was even better on the defense. She could zero in on whoever had the ball, and at one point, one of the humans actually turned and ran *from* her.

Halfway through the match, she also figured out that Grozz wasn't just being weird whenever he flailed a hand or moved his fingers strangely. He was using hand signals to point out players who were open or who possessed the Huttball. Once the two of them were in sync? Their team became *unstoppable*.

But then she rammed into the Iakaru too hard, knocking her to the floor roughly enough that she had trouble breathing for a moment. Rieve apologized, but the Iakaru waved it off. This wouldn't have bothered her, except moments later, a Rodian player on the other team tripped Rieve. At least, that was how it seemed to Rieve; it felt so *deliberate*. Was he angry at her for knocking down the Iakaru player?

She tried to keep her head in the game, but the Rodian targeted her every time no one was looking. Maybe he didn't like humans? At one point, he pinched her hard on the back of one of her arms, causing her to drop the Huttball.

It was a rough sport. She knew that. She *craved* that, if she was honest with herself. But this Rodian seemed to be specifically focusing on her. These pickup games were supposed to be a casual thing, yet her opponent was taking everything so seriously! Rieve did her best to ignore him, but finally, when he stomped on her foot to try to get her to fumble the Huttball, she snapped.

"What's your deal?" she shouted at him. "You got a problem?"

"What are you talking about?" he said, his hands up innocently. "I'm just playing the game."

Rieve's patience did not last much longer. When the Rodian spat on her neck during a particularly tough struggle, she decided she'd had enough. She shoved him so hard that he landed on his back. "Leave me *alone!*"

Grozz rushed up to Rieve. He howled something at her, his hand palm out and facing her.

"He keeps messing with me!" she explained.

Grozz brayed while nodding his head, and while his eyes looked sympathetic, the message was still clear to her: *Hey, calm* down*!*

Rieve looked to the others. That hungry joy she'd seen earlier?

Had been replaced with fear.

The magic of the game was gone in an instant. She didn't really belong there, did she? It reminded her how much she had struggled with Dragus's notion of teamwork. Rieve had her own reasons for playing Huttball, and she'd let them cloud her perspective.

She thanked Grozz for the opportunity, then jogged toward the exit of the Huttball arena. Grozz called after her, but she wouldn't look back. No. *Couldn't* look back. She was letting that voice in her head goad her into being rougher with the others. If she went too far . . .

She didn't want to think about that.

6

RIEVE'S SECOND DAY in the arena felt more or less like her first.

It didn't matter that she was well aware of how a Control match worked. She didn't realize until it was too late that she'd *never* trained in the Outpost battlefield, the one modeled after a traditional market square. This battlefield was mostly circular, compared with the longer ones she'd fought in before, which meant that in any given position, she could see the other Hunters.

She knew it would take practice, and she knew that eventually, she'd be able to ignore the arena crowds, but when was that day going to come? Her nerves spiked as she fought off Grozz, then Utooni, all before she made the exact same mistake.

Rieve let J-3DI get to her.

It wasn't even that big of a deal. But as she rolled out of the way of Grozz's weapons—which were actually two arms ripped from a droid's body—she heard J-3DI say something as his team captured the point:

"This is why you bring a Jedi along!"

No, she thought, *you're not a Jedi!*

She knew in hindsight that *that* was the moment the match was lost. Did she attack other members of the opposite team so they'd lose command of the control point, like she was supposed to? Did she listen to the frantic requests from her own teammates?

Or did she chase J-3DI around the battlefield for the remainder of the match?

Back in her prep pod, Rieve steamed. She'd had such high hopes for herself, but battling in the arena was proving to be a million times harder than she'd expected.

Dragus crept into her pod and knocked on the door after coming in. Rothwell was seeing to a small cut on her shoulder.

"Don't say it," she said.

Dragus smiled and grabbed the lapels of his red-and-black suit jacket. "Say what? I haven't even spoken."

"I know it's on the tip of your tongue."

"I have no idea what you're talking about."

"Teamwork," said Rieve. "You're going to tell me about teamwork."

"Wow, Rieve," he said, and sauntered over to her. "Did you use the Force to read my mind? However did you come up with that?"

"Dragus—"

"No, no," he said, his smile growing alongside his sarcasm. "I can't imagine *how* you guessed that correctly."

"Okay, okay, I get it," she said. "Cut me some slack."

"I am," he said. "It's your second day. The good thing about you messing up is that it's entertaining."

Rieve frowned. "Thanks. I guess?"

"I'm an entertainer, remember? I chose you because I knew you'd shake things up. We've never had someone like you in the arena before."

Rieve turned to the side so Dragus couldn't see her blushing.

Rothwell finished up with Rieve and dismissed himself politely, so Rieve started to gather up her stuff. "One more thing," said Dragus.

She narrowed her eyes at him.

"How do you feel about mornings?"

○ ○ ● ● ● ○ ○

The morning was wrong. Just as a concept. *Who invented the morning?* Rieve wondered. She had strong words for that person.

Not that anyone in Vespaara could tell it was morning when they stepped outside. The sky looked exactly the same as it had hours earlier, in the middle of the night. But as Rieve pulled the hood of her cloak tighter around her face, she felt it. In her bones. It was morning, and this time of the day was *wrong.*

But she had to be at the arena. Mandated by Dragus, actually. After her two awful performances in a row, he had said that he wanted to spend a little extra time training her on some specifics. She wasn't sure what that meant, but she had a guess. There'd be lots of ridiculous and pointless "team-building" exercises. She would probably be asked about her "feelings."

Her feelings were simple: she wanted to be in bed.

Rieve grunted at the security guard at the entrance to the arena and didn't even bother flashing her scandocs. She made straight for the chow room, located next to backstage. It was where all sorts of food, beverages, and other nutrition concerns could be addressed. And she had a concern that morning. She filled up a mug with caf and then, to the horror of the trainer who watched, she chugged the entire thing.

She slammed the mug down. "I'm awake now," she said.

Rieve changed into her more loose-fitting practice gear and was in the Outpost battlefield moments later, watching in dread as Dragus entered a few seconds after she got settled. He had on the same practice gear she did. It was odd seeing him in clothing that *wasn't* a ridiculous suit, but she realized he seemed to dress up only for match days.

And then she saw that J-3DI was right behind him.

"No, absolutely not," she said. "I thought you said you were going to train *me*."

"I am!" said Dragus. "But I can't do it alone because . . . well, that's the point."

"The best team in the arena is one that works together," said J-3DI matter-of-factly. "I am here to help you reconsider your battle tactics."

"My tactics are fine," she said. "Especially given how frequently you ran away from me last night."

"You remember how I told you I used to be a fighter?" asked Dragus.

"Sure. You were Durasteel. You used to fight—"

"In some underground fighting rings, yes," he said. "They were made up of one-on-one battles, Rieve. Your techniques? They would *thrive* there. You'd easily come out on top."

She sneered at J-3DI, as if to say, *I told you so*. He didn't react at all.

"But in this arena?" said Dragus. "With few exceptions, it's always four on four."

"Isn't that just one on one, but . . . four times over?"

He grimaced. "No, Rieve. Not remotely. And that's the problem. You're not thinking as part of a team."

"According to our understanding of history," said J-3DI, his voice excited and eager, "those who were Force-sensitive worked together as the Holy Order of the Jedi Knights to—"

"There are no Jedi anymore," she shot back. "There certainly aren't any here."

"Well, I am programmed for—"

"Did you intend for him to be so annoying?" said Rieve.

"Do *you* intend to be so annoying?" said Dragus, grinning.

Her mouth dropped open. "Me? I'm nothing like him!" she exclaimed, pointing at J-3DI.

"No, of course not," said Dragus. "You're a completely *different* kind of annoying."

She scowled at him. "What's the penalty if I hit you right now?"

Dragus didn't take the bait. He pointed to the raised section of the battlefield. "What happens if you end up on that side?"

"Why would I be up there?" said Rieve. "The control point is down here, and my weapon isn't long-range."

"Really? Because I seem to remember in your very first match, you deflected one of Sentinel's shots. And haven't you thrown that thing, too?"

The memory came back to her. She hadn't even thought about it at the time! She'd just thrown her lightsaber because it felt right.

"Oh," she said. "Yeah, I guess so."

"See?" he said. "You *can* think strategically. So, you know where in the arena your skills work best. But what happens if you get knocked out? Or the other team has lots of long-range fighters who are picking you off from up on the ridge?"

She grunted. "Well . . . I would go take them out. Simple as that."

"But *is* it?" Dragus shook his head. "What if Jay-Three is on your team? Is there anything you could do to take your challengers out while not abandoning the other two members of your team?"

Rieve scratched her head. She hadn't thought about it like that, and frustration started building in her. Why couldn't she just take them out and leave the other three behind?

"I believe that the best strategy would be working together," said J-3DI. "Our odds of success would increase."

"Okay, but *how*?" said Rieve. Then she turned to Dragus. "What could he possibly do to help?"

J-3DI answered the question before Dragus could. "As the resident Jedi Knight, I could execute a Force pull to bring a combatant to us so we could attack them in tandem."

"I could also take you apart piece by piece," she shot back.

"I don't think that would be wise."

"But it would be fun."

"Mostly for you. I think I would not like that."

"Well, why don't we try?"

"Are you two *children*?" said Dragus. "Rieve, listen to him. I know you don't buy his Jedi programming—"

"But I am a Jedi, Dragus," said J-3DI.

Dragus hesitated. "Sure," he said, then more to himself: "Gotta ask Sprocket to work on that protocol."

Rieve drew her lightsaber. "So, what you're saying is that I need to be . . . less impulsive?"

Dragus threw his hands in the air. "I can't believe it. You actually came to that conclusion yourself."

"I'll try to ignore how condescending that is," she said. "It's just . . . I don't know anyone. I don't know much about the other Hunters, either."

"Well, here's a good place to start," said Dragus. "Spend the next hour running drills with Jay-Three, but *actually* study his style."

"Because teamwork is the most important quality for a victory," said J-3DI. "The Jedi Order found it appropriate for masters to teach their Force-sensitive Padawans in the ways of—"

"Hold on. Do you see *me* as the Padawan in this scenario?" Rieve said.

J-3DI paused. "I suppose so."

"I don't even know what a Padawan *is*, but I'm definitely not that."

"Well, traditionally, the one who possesses more knowledge—"

Rieve groaned loudly. "Even though I'm a 'Sith Lord' in the arena, Dragus? Because I don't think a Sith Lord and a Jedi Knight would ever work together."

Dragus nodded. "Just because your character in the arena is a Sith doesn't mean you have to be antagonistic to *everyone*. You can still work with your team and be a Sith Lord to the other side."

"Those of us sensitive in the Force must always consider our actions beforehand," said J-3DI, nodding.

"You don't have Force sensitivity," said Rieve. "Trust me, you would feel differently about it if you did."

There was an awkward pause, and Dragus frowned. "What does *that* mean?"

She felt an odd prickling across her skin as panic started to bubble in her stomach. She'd said too much, and the voice in her head came back, telling her to run away, to leave this all behind like she always did.

Rieve shuddered. She would study the other Hunters, but those dark thoughts were a good reminder that she shouldn't *actually* get to know them. Having friends . . . that was a bad idea. Someday things would go sideways again, and she would run.

"Anyway, maybe we should do some of those drills," Rieve said, hoping to push past the awkwardness.

"Sure," said Dragus, who gave her an odd look but let it go.

J-3DI bowed in front of her. "I am ready to devote myself to your training, my Padawan," he said. "May the Force be through us."

Rieve groaned. "Not your Padawan!" she reminded him.

This was going to be a long hour.

**'VE GOT SOMETHING FOR YOU,"** said Rothwell as Rieve entered her prep pod that afternoon.

She sat in her chair and let Rothwell scan her with his medical device, which was wand-shaped and emitted a slight humming sound. He was quick to identify some muscles in her legs and arms that needed attention, which didn't surprise her. J-3DI turned out to be a lot spryer than she'd expected, and working with him during training that morning had wiped her out.

"Please tell me it's a new body," she groaned. "Just clone me or something. Have them go in the arena tonight in my place."

"Don't you have healing powers?" he asked. "I don't know how all this Force stuff works, honestly."

She shook her head. "It's not like that at all. Maybe it is for those who have more training than me, but I've never trained beyond what I've done alone. Do you think I'd need your help if I could heal myself?"

Rothwell chuckled at that as he returned, holding numerous audiochips. "I found some of these in the Backwater District," he said. "Thought you might like them."

She took them from Rothwell, who then began to massage out her sore spots. It was easy not to focus on the pain, though, because she couldn't believe what she was holding.

Each audiochip was a different gonkrock show.

There was Good Clone/Bad Clone at Yrdiel's. A set of Fall of the Empire at Reemo's Cantina on Nar Shaddaa. An entire week's worth of gigs from the Spires of Batuu, recorded from all over the system. And—

No way. No *way* was this possible.

Rieve read the text on the chip: *Corellia's Not Dead, The Blue Factory.*

It was her. That was *her* band.

"I assume they're okay?" said Rothwell. "I admit that I

don't know much about gonkrock. It's a little too chaotic for me, so I have no idea if these are any good, you know?"

"No, no, they're *perfect*," she said.

Rieve decided to indulge herself and handed Rothwell the audiochip with her old band on it. No one there knew about her past—either on Nar Shaddaa or in her hometown of Coronet City—so it didn't feel risky.

The drums rumbled. The chords rang out. And then . . . it was her. Screaming and barking and generally sounding like some sort of beast from Rakata.

She used it. She used it to get her mind into the right space for the upcoming battle. She needed to *be* a Sith Lord, to lean into the darker aspects of who she was to become that character, and the music . . . it helped her channel it all.

Rothwell helped Rieve dress, and she sat patiently while he applied her face makeup, then stretched out her muscles one last time.

"Thank you for that," she said. "It helped in ways you can't even imagine."

She swore he even blushed a little. "Just trying to be the

best trainer I can be," he said. "And I can't do that unless I figure out what makes you tick, you know?"

"True," she said, starting to head toward the tunnels.

"Before you go," said Rothwell. "Just one more thing."

She turned back. "What is it?"

He was quiet for a moment. "Just be careful," he said. "I've heard some mutterings back here. About you being the newcomer and all."

"I'll be fine," she said. "I'm going to try some of these 'teamwork' techniques that Dragus has been telling me about."

"Still," he said. "It's pretty tight-knit here, and you're new. An unpredictable element. I've seen how people react to those like you over the years."

"Thanks," she said, and she jogged toward the tunnel that would take her to the Ewok Village battlefield. Rothwell's words left her with an uncomfortable energy buzzing through her, but she was determined to make her mark in this place.

8

RIEVE REPEATED A SINGLE WORD in her head as the countdown in the player tunnel reached zero.

Teamwork. Teamwork. Teamwork.

That day was another first. Rieve hadn't fought in the Ewok Village before, but she saw there was an immediate advantage to it. The high platforms and trees made it easier to block out the sight of the stands, where countless fans of the Hunter fights cheered and screamed.

At the same time, she was still out of her element. Her team included Imara Vex and Zaina once more, but now Grozz roared alongside her as they all rushed the control point. They hadn't interacted much since she'd bailed on that Huttball scrimmage game. *Was Dragus right?* she wondered. *Do I really need to get to know my teammates better?* Maybe that would help her stop being so anxious around them.

There was no time to consider this at the present moment, though. The other team had reached the control point before Rieve's, so the four of them fell into offensive positions. Zaina and Imara Vex peeled off to get to higher vantage points while Zaina yelled over the comms, "Stick with Grozz, Rieve!"

"Yeah, yeah, I know," she muttered, but to be fair . . . she hadn't been able to stick with the goal of a match yet.

So she followed Grozz as the Wookiee raised one of his droid-arm weapons and slashed at Utooni. Rieve saw that Sentinel was setting up above them, which seemed to be his thing. He loved a good long-range attack.

You're starting to pick up on things, she thought.

She kept her lightsaber in a defensive position but wasn't sure where she should go next. Where was Slingshot or J-3DI? Her visibility was so limited in this battlefield and—

Grozz howled at her and she whipped around to see him doing something with his right hand.

"What?" she called out.

He pounded his chest and pointed up with a droid arm.

Wait. Was he——?

Oh. OH!

Grozz was using signals again, like he had in the Huttball arena! She gazed up and saw that Sentinel was repositioning his E-Web heavy repeater, which meant that she could anticipate where he was going to shoot.

She flung herself in front of Grozz just in time, allowing him to take out Utooni while she deflected repeater fire from Sentinel, who screamed out in frustration.

Grozz howled in victory but quickly gestured behind Rieve. She spun around to see Slingshot heading her way, and she wasted no time. She ducked behind one of the trees in the battlefield and managed to catch the Ugnaught. Rieve flung her lightsaber at him and cried out, "My enemies litter the battlefield!"

The other team never recovered, and for the first time, Rieve's team *won.*

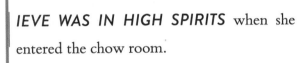

RIEVE WAS IN HIGH SPIRITS when she entered the chow room.

It helped that as soon as she stepped inside, Grozz rose from his seat and whooped loudly, calling out something that sounded like a war cry as he ran to her. He held her in a tight embrace—*Wow, he smells incredible. What do Wookiees bathe with?* she wondered—before the other Hunters also rose for a round of applause.

"That was an impressive feat you two pulled," said Aran Tal, the resident Mandalorian Hunter. He tapped the side of his beskar helmet with a finger. "Very cerebral."

"Um . . . sure," said Rieve, unsure how to deal with the compliment.

She wandered over to the hot food bar and grabbed some deep-fried nuna legs to munch on. There were tons of new foods to try on Vespaara, especially since there were so many different species on the planet. But deep-fried protein? That was good *anywhere* in the system.

Then she just watched.

It was easier than participating. She still didn't really know any of the Hunters, especially those on the second roster, since they rarely crossed paths with her roster. But watching them . . . a feeling rose in her that she couldn't recognize. She saw how easy it was for them to talk to one another. It was like . . . like she was back in Coronet City; she was the outsider at the orphanage all over again.

She hovered near one of the tables where Sentinel, Skora—the Rodian underworld medic—and Aran Tal were sitting. Both Sentinel and Skora were in street clothes instead of their arena costumes. Sentinel glanced at Rieve and briefly nodded at her, but then returned to his conversation. She looked at Grozz, who had drifted over to Zaina's table. That made sense.

Even out of the ring, Grozz had a hard time with Sentinel's past in the Empire.

Where did Rieve fit in either of these groups? She wasn't sure. So she put her knapsack on the floor next to her as she stood off to the side.

"You catch that podracing tournament last night?" Sentinel said.

"I prefer Huttball," muttered Aran Tal. "Much more physical."

Skora laughed. "That's just because your go-to outfit is a suit of armor."

"For the glory of Mandalore," he said. "Who am I to buck tradition?"

"Oh, come on," said Sentinel. "You're just afraid that you won't be any good without all that beskar."

"Why do you care so much, bucket brain? Worried you might get a little jealous of my superior fighting skills?"

"I'm as cool as a dead star," said Sentinel, scratching at the dark stubble on his chin. "And *you* are distracting us from the real issue. Maybe you and I should face off sometime."

"You can't handle either of us," said Skora. "What are you without that heavy repeater?"

"Whatever," said Sentinel.

Rieve smiled at that, at how effortless it was for them to crack jokes. She still didn't participate, though. It was always easier to observe. Yet her attention started to drift when Sentinel and Skora began arguing fiercely about whose home planet was superior. She had a nuna leg in her mouth when she realized that Sentinel had said her name.

"Huh?" She swallowed quickly, probably *too* quickly, and nearly choked. "What?"

"I said that you seem pretty quiet over there," he said. "What's your story?"

"Yeah," said Skora. "I didn't see a personal history attached to your Hunter profile."

"I didn't provide one," said Rieve. "Didn't realize it was needed."

"Well, maybe not *needed*," said Sentinel, "but you can tell us anything. Can't promise that we'll control our reactions, but eventually we forget even the most embarrassing stories." He snickered. "Except for Zaina's, that is. We like to tease her about her civilian life before she came to Vespaara. Isn't that right, Zaina?"

Zaina didn't even look Sentinel's way. "Not taking the bait!" she called out.

A voice rang out clear in Rieve's head:

Will they ever be your friends if they know the truth? If they know what you did?

She pushed past it. "I grew up on Corellia. In Coronet City."

"I spent time there!"

Rieve twisted around to see Tuya, the blue-skinned Twi'lek slicer, come springing into the chow room. She was shorter than most of the other Hunters, but she made up for that with a bouncy, chaotic energy and her incredible hacking skills. Her two head tails—called lekku—were draped over her blue-and-green outfit, and her droid assistant, T-U8, buzzed near her head.

"Really?" said Rieve. "It's nothing special. It's like any big city in the Core Worlds, I guess."

"I liked it there," said Tuya. "Fun people, those Corellians. A lot of them were very helpful when I ran missions there to steal Imperial data."

"So, you come from Corellia," said Sentinel, trying to redirect the conversation. "And you're clearly not a *real* Sith Lord."

That stung, but Rieve was quick with a comeback. "You're clearly not a puppet of the Empire anymore. Or are you?"

Sentinel rose immediately, but Skora reached out an arm to stop him.

"Got a slick mouth on you, do ya?" he said.

"I've got a mean backhand, as well," she shot back. "Wanna find out about that, too? We can discuss my history all day."

"Sentinel, come *on*," said Zaina from her table nearby. "She's been here . . . what? A month? Cut her some slack."

"I don't need my hand to be held, rebel wannabe," snapped Rieve.

And then *his* voice echoed through the chow room.

J-3DI's.

"Well, you certainly have much to learn, my young apprentice."

"'Apprentice'?" Rieve wanted to leap over the table and throttle J-3DI. "I am *not* a Jedi, and I am certainly *not* your apprentice. Didn't we discuss that already?"

"Well, we *did* train together quite hard this morning," said J-3DI, in that cheery know-it-all tone of his. "I think you're showing real improvement, young one!"

"Aren't you like three weeks old?" Rieve shouted. "I've got over twenty *years* on you!"

Grozz laughed and pounded the table repeatedly.

Rieve could feel it building again: with more chaotic emotions came that instability. The Force surged within, and she looked in shock at the nuna legs she held.

They were levitating oh so slightly above the plate.

She tossed the food and grabbed her knapsack from the floor. She could trade verbal jabs with Sentinel and J-3DI all day, but this was becoming too risky. Rieve was out of her element, in an environment that was still too new to her.

"Don't leave," said Zaina. "Come on! They were just fooling around."

"It's fine," said Rieve. "I have things to do."

"Just *staaaaay*," said Tuya. "We are as welcoming as we are insulting! And I have at least thirty-five more questions to ask you about Corellia."

"Maybe next time," said Rieve.

Zaina chuckled. "Is one of your other powers running away when things get difficult?"

At heart, Rieve knew Zaina meant that as a joke. She knew it! And yet she turned and glared at Zaina. A hundred different bitter insults were on the tip of her tongue.

Don't burn this bridge yet, Rieve, she told herself, fighting what the *other* voice was telling her.

Which was to burn it all down.

Maybe Rothwell had been right. Did these people see her as an outsider and nothing more? Would they *always* see her that way, since she was the last member added to the roster?

She left the room without another word.

*UST AS RIEVE KNEW IN HER BONES* when it was morning, she also knew when it was night.

She preferred the night to the day, and that made being on Vespaara challenging sometimes, what with its never-changing twilight. Still, as she left the arena, that familiar itch ran through her.

It was nighttime, and she wanted to *be* somewhere.

Rieve had grown up on the streets of Coronet City. She had a curfew at the orphanage she lived in, but it wasn't long before the Togruta sisters who ran the place realized that Rieve was never, *ever* going to follow the rules. As long as she returned to her bed at some point and kept herself out of trouble, they stopped bothering her.

So the idea of staying in at night did not appeal to Rieve. It was simply not her style.

After leaving the arena, Rieve stopped by home first. Her small bungalow was modest, just big enough for her to sleep and wash up. It had a small stove built into the counter, but she rarely used it, since she ate most of her meals at work. Truthfully, she really only slept there, just like she used to do back at the orphanage. That was all a home was good for, right?

Rieve dropped off her knapsack and splashed water on her face. Then she headed out to do what she knew best: get into some trouble.

Rieve's home was on a long block of similar bungalows, and Sentinel lived across from her, but he was always coming or going, too, so she'd only been able to wave or nod at him before he disappeared. She threw the hood of her cloak over her head and joined the crowd of partiers, tourists, and arena fans, blending in as if she was nobody, not a Hunter in Balada the Hutt's arena.

With no destination in mind, she let the flow of the crowd guide her. Any number of languages rang out around her as she walked. Vespaara brought more than just tourists. There were lots of gamblers. People looking for entertainment. Smugglers. Some of the brightest, most ambitious people and those you might find under a barrel-scrub. Vespaara was the new get-rich-quick scheme come to life, and people were flocking to it.

It had also brought Rieve. She felt good about what she'd done in the arena that day, but it was hard for her to avoid the nagging sensation that her first victory in a match was a fluke. After all, she'd succeeded on Nar Shaddaa for a solid run, all before . . .

Stop it, she told herself. *Stop obsessing over the past.*

Rieve pushed down her prickling nerves and the horrible images that came with it. She had made it to Balada's arena, and she just needed to focus, keep her head down, and release some energy now and again. Besides, it wasn't like there was anywhere else she could go on Vespaara. The southern pole was the only habitable location.

And she certainly couldn't return to her original home.

Rieve turned off the main strip toward the long line of music venues and cantinas in what was known as the Backwater District. It was like her spirit knew exactly where she needed to go. *Maybe it's the Force,* she thought. She'd never had any official training in this mysterious, seemingly mystical thing she felt, but she knew it had helped her to be a talented courier on Corellia. After Coronet City, she had experimented with it. Tested its boundaries and her own limitations. And every so often, it seemed to speak to her. On the whole, she had a sense of what it allowed her to do.

And what happened when she lost control.

Rieve turned down another darkened road, one with less foot traffic, and the sudden squeal of feedback set her heart racing in anticipation. Was that—? No. It couldn't be.

A drumbeat galloped to life, and Rieve couldn't believe her ears. A real-life gonkrock band! There! On Vespaara! Seconds later, she stood outside of an establishment called the Oasis Cantina, and beyond the doorless entrance, she could see a band setting up on a stage in the back of the room. She was so thrilled by the sight that she didn't hear someone calling out her name until they were nearly upon her.

"Is that you, Rieve?"

Rieve turned around to see Zaina, Imara Vex, and Grozz approaching. In the moment, she was torn. Should she just dart inside the Oasis Cantina and pretend she didn't hear them? This wasn't necessarily something she wanted to share with her fellow Hunters.

But they'd already said her name, and they were too close, so Rieve raised a reluctant hand to wave at them. "Hey," she said, "what are you all doing here?"

Zaina gestured at Grozz. "He wanted to get up to something rowdy, so I figured Backwater was the place to be." She pointed at the entrance to the Oasis Cantina. "You come here before?"

The drummer proceeded to bang on her multilayer kit, testing out the sound system, and Rieve looked nervously back and forth between the cantina and the Hunters. "No," she admitted. "Never been inside. I just thought it sounded like something I might like."

"Gonkrock, right?" said Imara Vex, smiling. "I knew a bounty hunter years ago who loved the stuff, so I'm a little familiar."

"Well, let's go in," said Zaina. "Grozz, you in for a loud and violent night?"

Grozz nodded vigorously and howled his approval.

"Wait, really?" said Rieve, her heart skipping a beat. "You like this stuff?"

"Oh, honey, I don't know the first thing about it," confessed Zaina. "I'm more into the older stuff: droidpop and electro-twang. But you gotta live dangerously, right?"

Zaina flashed her scandocs at the door—all employees of any of the entertainment facilities on Vespaara had unlimited access to the others—and then she pushed her way forward. Imara Vex shrugged and followed her, and Grozz—Grozz looked like he was going to explode from excitement.

Here goes nothing, thought Rieve.

She made her way inside the cantina, past arms and tentacles and other appendages, until she was closer to the stage, alongside the other three Hunters. The band consisted of three members. There was a tall Anx male with a rumble bass stage left, and his blade-shaped head crest changed colors as he tuned his instrument. A human female with purple hair sat behind the massive cluster drum kit, and a Xexto—a tall, six-limbed species with gangly appendages—was perfectly suited to the mechanical dual guitar.

Rieve worried that she was revealing too much. What if they thought she was too strange for them? What if they had a bad time and blamed it on her? She was antsy and nervous, which seemed to defeat the whole purpose of her night out in the first place. How would she release the energy building in her if she was being watched?

The trio of musicians onstage struck out a few notes together, and the crowd surged, pushing forward, crying out in anticipation. In that instant, Rieve's worries washed away, because she missed this. She missed what it felt like to be packed into a room like canned burra fish with people who sought the same release. The loud, vicious chords rang out, pushed deeper by the bass and the drums, and the crowd raised their various appendages around Rieve, chanting out something she didn't recognize, but it didn't matter. You didn't need to be in the know there. You just had to let yourself go.

And then *he* stepped onstage.

He was dressed in a long maroon robe that dragged behind him. His head was shaved, and his normally brown face was covered in red and gold makeup that gave him the appearance of something terrifying and powerful. Yet even in costume, Rieve recognized him in an instant.

Yemar, the drummer of the band she had abandoned on Nar Shaddaa, now trying his hand at vocal duties.

"Are you ready to give up your souls tonight, Vespaara?" Yemar called out, and the crowd cheered in response.

I have to leave, Rieve thought, but Zaina grabbed her arm and jumped up and down.

"This is already amazing!" she said, and that was when the first song hit them all like a Star Destroyer crashed into the building.

Yemar barked at them in a voice she had *never* heard him use when she sang for Corellia's Not Dead, and the band thrashed about onstage, matching the energy the crowd was giving them. Rieve felt terror building in her. It was only a matter of time before Yemar saw her, and then what? What would he do to the person who'd caused the end of his previous band?

What would he do to the person who'd just disappeared overnight?

Imara Vex—surprising Rieve—was pointing at Yemar and singing his lyrics right back at him, and Grozz was slack-jawed as he towered over most of the people in the audience. He turned and looked at Rieve. Without a word, he raised his thumb in the air.

Well, at least he likes it, she thought.

She planned her escape. She'd wait for a break in the set, and then she'd excuse herself to the bathroom. Maybe she could start a fight and use that to get out of the Oasis Cantina. *Any* distraction would work right now, and—

"Stop the music! Stop it!"

The instruments came to an abrupt stop, and when Rieve

looked up, Yemar was making direct eye contact with her.

"Rieve? Is that you?"

Her heart sank to her feet. No, no, this couldn't be happening. She couldn't let these people find out what she'd done!

"Folks, we have a special treat in the house tonight," continued Yemar, and then he extended his hand. "Rieve, join an old friend onstage, will you?"

"What?" she said.

"Wait, is he talking to you?" asked Zaina.

Yemar hopped off the stage, and the crowd parted immediately. He went toward her, his arms outstretched, and soon he had her in a tight hug.

"I missed you," he said, not into the microphone in his hand but into her ear. "Please do this for me."

She pulled away and looked him in the face, and the truth was that she had missed him, too. A lot. Yemar, Ully, and Boornan, all of whom had made up Corellia's Not Dead with her, who had given Rieve another life for a few years before she'd left them.

Zaina's words echoed in her head:

But you gotta live dangerously, right?

So Rieve nodded at her old friend.

Yemar took her hand and guided her up on the stage amid the confusion and anticipation of the crowd, and from up there, above the audience, so many memories of her time in a band flooded back.

"Folks, years ago I was in a band with Rieve here, which some of you know. How many of you listened to Corellia's Not Dead?"

To Rieve's surprise, a solid portion of the crowd screamed up at the stage.

"Rieve," said Yemar, "would you do us the favor of singing? Just one song? For the old days."

The audience cheered and applauded for her, and she saw Grozz pumping his fist in the air.

She had gone there for a release.

And in its own strange way, the universe had provided for her.

"'Forever,'" she said. "You remember that song?"

Yemar flashed her a toothy grin. "I'll never forget it."

He nodded at the drummer, and a stage tech rushed up to hand Rieve a microphone. Like the moment when Rothwell had given her a lightsaber, she felt like a piece of her had been returned to her body. It just felt *right*.

"It's been a while," she said to the crowd, "so forgive me."

The roar of the crowd was cut off by a frantic drumbeat, and then the rush came: The memories of being onstage. The lyrics. The joy and release that came from spilling out all your emotions to a bunch of strangers.

So Rieve sang. She sang about how Coronet City would always belong to the people, how the Empire would never be able to outlast them, and it all built to a brutal breakdown where the call-and-response refrain sent the entire building into a frenzy.

"*It will be ours!*" she growled out.

And the people below screamed back at her: "*FOREVER!*"

She lost herself in the music, pulled back to reality only when she saw Grozz crowd-surfing over the surging bodies. Giving herself to the moment, she dove into the crowd, held up by countless hands and other appendages as she crawled over to Grozz, sang to him, then thrashed her way back to the stage.

When the final chord rang out, the room erupted in noise. Rieve nearly broke into laughter when she saw that both Zaina and Imara Vex stood off to the side, their mouths hanging open.

She'd taken a risk, and it had been utterly worth it.

Back at home, she struggled to fall asleep. She replayed the night in her head, especially the look on Yemar's face when she'd approached him after his band's set was over. He'd told her that they were rushing off Vespaara to catch a gig on the nearest planet but that he would come back. He wanted to catch up with Rieve and find out what she'd been up to.

"Sure," she said. "And . . . we should talk. About . . . you know."

He nodded. "I'd like that."

That surprised her. So did the reaction from Zaina, Imara Vex, and Grozz. They might not have expected what they experienced at the Oasis Cantina, but none of them ran from her screaming. If anything, they genuinely seemed *more* interested in her.

But as she tried to find sleep, the same thought kept repeating in her mind:

This won't last.

 **LEASE TELL ME THIS IS A JOKE,"** said Rieve.

"Unfortunately, it's not," said Rothwell as he wiped a towel across his face.

"There's no airflow in the pod?"

"Nope."

"Literally none."

"None. It's like a sauna in there."

She sighed. "What happened?"

Rothwell guided Rieve into her humid, sweltering prep pod. "We don't know, but the air circulation unit went down a few hours ago. They've got techs working on it now."

She groaned. "Well, at least we're all suffering."

Rothwell winced. "Um . . . not technically."

She dropped her knapsack on the floor next to the med chair. "What's *that* supposed to mean?"

"Well," he said, drawing the word out. "It's only *your* pod that's down, Rieve."

"You're kidding," she said, closing her eyes.

"Wasn't kidding before, either. Can't you just . . ." He waved his hand over the prep pod. "I don't know. Force it fixed?"

"It doesn't work like that. In my experience it mostly controls you, not the other way around. Can't we use another one?" she asked, upset that she had *already* started sweating.

"All occupied," he said. "There are sixteen Hunters, and this place currently only has capacity for sixteen pods."

She threw herself into the chair. "Let's get this over with as quick as possible," she said. "We'll do the makeup in the main area, because there's no way it's sticking now with this much sweat."

As Rothwell worked quickly, Rieve wondered if someone was playing a prank on her. She *was* the newbie, and hazing wasn't out of the question. Maybe this was their way of reminding Rieve that she still had to prove herself.

That just annoyed her more.

"How do you do this, Rothwell?"

Rothwell looked up from wrapping Rieve's legs with the med tape. "Do this?" he said, gesturing to her legs. "It's not *that* complicated. It's tape."

"No, not *that*," she said. "This. Being a trainer. Is this what you always wanted to do?"

He stared at her for a moment, studying her face. Then he looked away and sighed. "Honestly, no," he said. "I had other dreams. Other things I wanted to do."

Rieve recognized that hesitancy in an instant. It was the same thing she'd felt the previous day when Sentinel asked her for her story. So she decided not to pry, but surprisingly, Rothwell kept talking.

"I got into this mostly out of desperation," he continued.

"Something happened a long time ago. I had to leave home. It was a very sudden thing. And once I was safe, I basically picked up what work I could."

"Whatever helped you survive," she said softly.

Rothwell looked up at her. "Yeah. Yeah, that exactly." He moved to her other leg. "Sounds like you have an idea what that's like."

"Maybe," she said.

"Well, I picked up some things here and there. Studied medicine and physical therapy for a bit, and I worked for a fighting ring on Chandar's Folly."

"A fighting ring?" She raised an eyebrow at that, then brushed some sweat from her temple. "So you're used to this kind of chaos, huh?"

He laughed. "I guess so. But my life before that . . . it was more chaotic. This?" He gestured to the backstage area beyond the prep pod. "Much more stable."

Rieve hesitated.

"Do you ever miss it?"

Rothwell tilted his head to the side in confusion.

"Before," she clarified. "Whatever you used to do. Or wherever you came from."

He continued to wrap the rest of her leg, then stood up and patted it gently. "Every day," he said. "I'd take it all back in an instant if I could."

Rothwell helped Rieve into her outfit, and she couldn't stop the words from leaving her mouth.

"I sometimes wonder if this is what I'm supposed to do."

"Fight?"

"Sure. Or be here. In the arena."

He frowned. "Do you *like* fighting?"

"I do, actually!" she said, nodding her head. "It's a great release of energy, and I think I'm pretty good at it."

"Well, don't tell anyone I said this," said Rothwell, leaning close to her, "but sometimes I wonder if Balada the Hutt and Dragus aren't holding you back."

She jerked away from him, by instinct more than anything else. "What?"

Rothwell put his hands up, a gesture of innocence. "I'm just saying. All these rules and strategies! I saw you those first couple of days. When you seek out a target, you're brutal. Efficient. *I* wouldn't reel that in."

"Well, Dragus wants me to focus on teamwork, remember?" said Rieve.

Rothwell handed Rieve her lightsaber, and she gave it a few test swings. "Sure," he said. "I mean, I get that. But I see the way the others look at you."

Rieve frowned. "How? What do you mean?"

"Like you're a child," he said simply.

They didn't speak as they stepped out of her prep pod, and she was thankful for the rush of cold air. Rieve hoped the pod would be repaired soon. She was patient with Rothwell while he used a portable hand fan to cool her off, then set her makeup once he'd applied it on her face.

Her teammates didn't say much to her, and they certainly didn't mention her broken ACU. Grozz, Imara Vex, and Zaina didn't even say anything about the previous night.

So this had to be a joke, right?

It was the only thing on Rieve's mind as she stood with her teammates at the Hunters' entrance to one of the battlefields.

But then she wondered: *was* she being held back?

12

**O**NCE RIEVE GOT ON THE battlefield, though, all her nervous thoughts disappeared.

Despite the fact that the entire arena had perfect climate controls, she still felt a chill as she ran into Frontline, the Hoth battlefield. Maybe it was psychological, or maybe Balada the Hutt had designed it so the environment would feel as real as possible.

No matter, though, because Rieve was trying to focus not just on reaching the control point but on figuring out how to work with Sentinel, who was on her team for the day. They'd always opposed each other in the past, so Rieve tried to remember what Dragus had taught her.

How could Rieve's style work well with Sentinel's?

Grozz reached the control point first, and interpreting his hand signals felt like second nature now. He waved Imara Vex to provide him cover on one side of the point but sent Sentinel and Rieve to the opposite end. She noticed that Grozz—who generally didn't care for Sentinel and *loved* whacking him with his droid arms when Sentinel was on the other team—didn't seem to be at all bothered by his presence. He had already adapted.

Okay, so why did he want her to work with Sentinel? What was he seeing?

Moments later, it was so obvious that Rieve was a bit ashamed she hadn't seen it herself. Sentinel set up his repeater to send a barrage of blasts down on anyone who came close to them, and she realized it was the perfect distraction. No one would expect Rieve to sneak up on them and take them out.

It worked. Over and over again. The two of them managed to take out Zaina, Slingshot, and Utooni, with the latter failing *twice* to take possession of the control point.

Grozz roared out a warning near the end of the match, and Rieve spotted J-3DI making a last-minute play to knock out Sentinel. She rushed toward the droid, and he whirled his head around to spot her. He brought his blue lightsaber up to block, but her attacks were too focused, too quick, and she felt a rush of joy as she realized she was about to take him out. He tried to nab her with his mechanized arm as his hand shot out toward her, but she dodged it easily.

She raised her lightsaber up.

She brought it down.

And *nothing* connected with J-3DI.

Literally nothing. She swung her lightsaber again, and a cry rose from the stands, because they'd realized what had happened, too.

There was no plasma blade emitting from the hilt.

She stared down at it, panic welling in her chest.

"Rieve?" said J-3DI. "What are you doing?"

The chime-bell rang out, announcing the end of the match.

Rieve's team had won, but . . . she hadn't shut off her

lightsaber. She pressed her thumb over the activation switch, over and over and—

Nothing.

Nothing at all.

IN THE DARKNESS, *he flipped on his datapad, and the stream from the holonet came to life.*

"But here comes Rieve," said L-X1, one of the announcers, "and she seems to be making a direct play for Jay-Threedeeaye."

He watched as Rieve rushed the Jedi Knight droid.

"Ever since Rieve's debut," said Boz Vega, "this rivalry has been relentless! Reminds me of back in my day, when Hril the Great used to treat me like his personal punching bag and—"

He smiled. He couldn't help it.

"Boz, are you seeing what I'm seeing?"

"Did she—"

The announcers were speechless for a moment, and it filled him with an immense joy.

"Where is her lightsaber?" asked Boz Vega.

"She's still holding it, Boz. She appears to be examining it. Are we seeing an equipment malfunction?"

"Perhaps this is just an amateur mistake," mused Boz. "The match has come to an end, and the Mudhorns have won, but that's gotta be an embarrassing victory for Rieve, who is just . . ."

"She's just standing there," finished L-X1.

It was perfect.

Because it had begun.

 **IEVE TOSSED HER LIGHTSABER** down on the metal table in front of Rothwell, and the clang echoed loudly.

"What just happened?" she demanded. "How could it just go *off*?"

"I have no idea, Rieve," said Rothwell, picking it up. "I'll run diagnostics on it, take it apart."

"Is it a faulty blade emitter? The activator switch? Something else?" She stepped closer to Rothwell. "Because I can't be embarrassed like that in the arena again!"

"Look, we won," said Imara Vex, coming up alongside her. "Just accept the victory and move on."

Rieve waved at her dismissively. "It could have been better. *I* could have been better."

Imara Vex shrugged and wandered off, clearly uninterested in arguing Rieve's point. Rothwell flipped the lightsaber a few times and tried to activate it, but it still wouldn't turn on.

"Maybe I should talk to Balada," he said.

"Why?" Rieve asked.

"Well, she *is* the one who 'collected' all the weapons and gear the Hunters use in the arena."

Rieve looked down at her outfit. "Even *this*?"

He nodded. "And Jay-Threedeeaye's lightsaber has never malfunctioned." Rothwell shrugged. "Maybe Balada shouldn't be so careless about what she brings here. You never know what it might do."

"First the ACU, then this?" Rieve sighed in exasperation. "I really am the runt here, aren't I?"

Rothwell shrugged, then turned away and disappeared into the network of tunnels.

At least Rothwell was supporting her. When she turned

to leave backstage, Dragus called out her name. "You're not leaving yet," he said.

"That sounds like a demand, not a question," she said, and then let out a loud groan.

"Good job today," he said, slightly out of breath. "Honestly."

"Thanks," she said, and she began to remove the med tape from her arms. "Could have done better."

"A malfunction like that has no bearing on your actual talent, okay?"

She smiled sarcastically at him. "So . . . what do you need? I kinda want to get out of here. My prep pod's ACU is *still* busted."

"It'll be fixed, I promise," he said. "I have a surprise for you."

"A surprise?"

"Yep."

"I don't know that I like surprises from you, Dragus," she said. "Is it the identity of whoever played a prank on me? Because that's two things 'malfunctioning' in a row."

"Prank?" Dragus scowled. "No one's pranking you, Rieve."

"Whatever," she said. "What's the surprise?"

○ ○ ● ● ● ○ ○

Rieve stood in the Outpost battlefield the next morning, and she swore if Dragus ever told her he had a surprise for her again, she would destroy him on the spot.

She pulled back the hood on her cloak and marveled at the outfit Dragus was wearing: tight, formfitting clothing and armored gloves. What was he thinking?

"I don't like you anymore," she told him, rubbing at her eyes.

"I didn't say it was a *good* surprise," he countered. "Ah, here come our competitors for the day."

Rieve turned around to see J-3DI and Grozz strolling up, the two chatting rapidly in Shyriiwook.

"What is this, Dragus?" she said. "We gonna play a little two-on-two Huttball?"

Grozz howled in excitement.

"Actually, hold on to that thought," said Dragus. "But no,

not today. You and I . . . we're going to do a little bit more training, and I recruited these two to help us."

"Help us what?" said Rieve. "I thought you said I did good yesterday!"

He stepped closer as he wrapped a med band around his forehead. "You did. I wasn't lying. That doesn't mean you can't get *better*."

"At what?"

"There are many paths to self-improvement," said J-3DI. "Would you like more information on how you can use your sensitivity to the Force to your advantage? I have plenty of—"

"I'm fine," said Rieve.

"Maybe some other time," said Dragus, nodding his head at J-3DI. "Right now, let's do some drills, then you and I will face off against these two tree-goats."

"I am not a tree-goat," said J-3DI. "I am a Jedi Knight."

Rieve ignored this because she was much more interested in what Dragus had just said. "I'm sorry, *you* are going to fight with *us*?"

"I can't be a good manager if I don't get a little dirty, right?" Dragus said. "Plus, I might be older, but I'm certainly not any less talented."

Grozz groaned at him.

"Just wait, Grozz," said Dragus. "I'm sure I'll surprise you."

At that, Dragus took off at a dead sprint up the ramp that led to the higher platforms in the Outpost battlefield.

"I don't like his surprises," Rieve muttered. She turned to Grozz. "Do *you* like his surprises?"

Grozz shrugged, then headed to the opposite side of the battlefield.

Their training was brutal, not just because it was so physical. Grozz knocked her down twice, and J-3DI managed to pull her closer to him with that aggravating move of his. She just couldn't seem to concentrate. Dragus wanted her to focus on where he was at all times so she wouldn't be so prone to going off on her own. "You've gotten better at this in a short length of time," Dragus told her in between rounds. "But when it's happened in the arena, someone else led *you*. I want to see you start leading others in a plan of attack."

"Can that plan of attack involve a nap?" she huffed out.

"Eventually. But for now?" He pointed toward J-3DI and Grozz. "Imagine we're in a Control match. Those two are coming for you. What's your strategy?"

She shrugged. "Knock them out?"

"Okay, yes, but *how*?"

"I don't know! Normally, I have a lightsaber, and I do my best to swing it toward a target really fast!" She threw her hands up in the air. "Do I have to remind you that I'm not an *actual* Sith Lord again?"

"But you need to *look* like one," Dragus said. He whistled loudly, then called out to the other Hunters. "Come and get us!"

"We don't have a plan, Dragus!" she said.

"No, *you* don't," he said. "*I* have at least ten plans."

Grozz and J-3DI sprinted in their direction.

"Because you just react, Rieve. You wait until the moment, and then you choose to do something without considering what your options are."

Grozz's longer stride meant he'd pulled ahead of J-3DI, and he was even closer.

"But I need you to start observing and *then* attacking."

"What is wrong with you?" screamed Rieve, holding her arms up in a defensive posture.

"Absolutely everything," said Dragus, smiling.

Grozz roared as he came upon them and raised one hand high. He swung down at Dragus.

Rieve almost didn't see Dragus move because he was *that* quick. He darted out of the path of Grozz's arm, then immediately walloped Grozz on his side. The Wookiee wheezed and doubled over.

"See, Grozz favors his right side," said Dragus, "so if you let him swing at you, he's exposed. A perfect opportunity."

J-3DI was next, and his hands spun with mechanical precision as he tried to take down Dragus. But Dragus was way ahead of him, and after dodging a flurry of attacks, he swept his leg out and sent J-3DI into the air.

"If you watch Jay-Three, you'll realize how proficient and brilliant he is," said Dragus, barely breathing hard after that impressive display. "But only at what he knows. He's programmed with a lot, but not *everything*. The element of surprise works best on him."

"I did not sense through the Force what you were about to do," said J-3DI, pushing himself up. "That was an excellent strategy."

"A fighter will reveal a lot about themselves if you just pay attention," said Dragus.

"So if you can do *that*," said Rieve, "why don't you fight anymore?"

Dragus helped up a still wheezing Grozz. "I prefer being behind the scenes. There's somethin' about training a fighter that is more satisfying than actually doing it. This is Balada's arena, remember? She owns all this. So I get to be the public face of the Hunters and I don't have to fight in the arena myself. It's like the best of both worlds."

Then he glanced at Grozz, who softly moaned and rubbed his side.

"And it's a much less painful way to make a boatload of credits," Dragus added.

Rieve laughed at that. "Okay, so what's next?"

"Practice," he said.

She groaned. "I was afraid you were going to say that."

"It's simple, but there's a reason it works." He paused for a moment. "It won't hurt you to get to know your teammates better. I know this is a competitive arena, but we gotta make sure that the fans are getting their money's worth."

"Okay," she said, but that was mostly to shove her discomfort away and get past the moment. Dragus was really pushing her to get to know the other Hunters, at least in a tactical sense. It seemed like a lot of work.

But . . . would they continue asking questions about her? She was certain that Imara Vex or Zaina would eventually interrogate her about her lead singer past, but so far at least they seemed fine with it. What if one of them found out what had happened on Corellia?

No. No, that couldn't happen.

The images appeared in her head, sudden, unwelcome.

The man in the dark cloak.

The alley.

The stormtroopers.

She immediately started sweating. "So, let's try again," she said to Dragus. "Me and you against these two tree-goats."

"Again, I must remind you that I'm a Jedi Knight," said J-3DI.

She smiled ear to ear. "Then prove it."

Rieve tried her best to imagine herself beating J-3DI again. But as they ran drill after drill, she couldn't escape the memory. It was like a blaze bug, biting her over and over again, and the voice reminded her why:

They're going to find you, it said.

And then your new friends . . . they're all going to abandon you, just like you've abandoned everyone you've ever known.

She swung at Grozz and missed.

Which is exactly what you deserve.

He knocked her down.

Just run away. Far, far away.

Rieve felt completely off track at the end of practice, but Dragus still thanked her.

"What for?" she asked. "Wait, did I have a choice about coming to this?"

He laughed. "Not really. But I do appreciate you giving it a dedicated effort."

"Well, I'll appreciate if you never make me wake up early again," she said. "And what did you mean earlier? The whole Huttball thing?"

"You gave me an idea," he said. "Tomorrow, first match in the arena: the Hunters play Huttball in the Gauntlet battlefield."

"Really?" She liked that idea. And maybe she could knock J-3DI down on his smug—

"You ready to smash some heads?" he asked.

At least Rieve had something to look forward to.

14

**IEVE HAD BEEN ON HER OWN** since her days in the orphanage. Once she got to Vespaara, there'd been so much prep work, especially while she was training, that she hadn't had much time to herself. But there wasn't a match in the arena that night so the techs could perform necessary maintenance to keep the place up to Balada's standards. Which meant that Rieve had her first day off since she'd arrived on this strange planet.

Unfortunately, the timing couldn't have been worse. Rieve felt anxious and untethered after her training session, and she needed the arena to burn off all her excess energy.

Because if she didn't . . .

She tried to nap. It didn't work. She was too restless. After hours of pointless tossing and turning, she showered, slipped on clothes and her cloak, and rushed out of her home, met by the red-and-purple skies of Vespaara.

This time, she headed toward the Arena District, where all three competitive arenas sat, sparkling in the Vespaara skyline. She thought about trying Huttball again, but the idea of partnering up with *anyone* at that moment seemed pointless. So she strolled up to the entrance of the podracing arena.

Most of the other Hunters preferred Huttball to podracing, but she'd seen Dizzy working on a podracer kit for his droideka backstage after the previous match. Incredibly, the results were super realistic. But she didn't think she'd see him near the track, which was better for Rieve. She was too much in her head to maintain any sort of conversation with another person.

Rieve hoped the energy of the crowd would be just what she needed. She flashed her scandocs and kept her head down as she wove among all the patrons scurrying to catch the next race. She pushed through a long line at concessions, where attendees were buying all sorts of fried and sweet snacks, like the nuna legs she'd had the other day and meiloorun fruit, which was immensely popular on Vespaara. She found a set of stairs into the seats, and up and up into the stands she went, past the clumps of fans, families, and tourists, until she was able to get a seat mostly to herself at the top of the arena.

Podracing had been outlawed long, long before, but out there, in the Outer Rim, no one really cared. Rieve wasn't sure anyone from the New Republic even knew what was happening on this planet. She watched as all the podracers climbed into their vehicles and the crowd began to whoop up a fury, anxious for the race to start. The roar swelled with the countdown, and then they were off, racing across the natural black sand of Vespaara, which made the podracers stand out sharply. Even she got a little caught up in that first lap.

But then her mind wandered back to the Hunters' arena. It had to be a good sign that Dragus wanted to continue training her. Or was that a sign that he thought she wasn't cutting it?

Maybe it was Balada the Hutt who wasn't sure about her. It *was* Balada's arena, after all, and while Dragus was partnered with the Hutt, the whole thing was ultimately her creation. Rieve couldn't tell one way or another, especially since Balada was always up in her ship or skipping through the galaxy in search of the next thing for her collection.

Did these people even want her there?

No one wants you.

She tried to ignore it. Tried to ignore the needling sensation over her skin as her heart rate sped up. What was she doing there? Was she going to fight a bunch of strangers until she couldn't anymore? Would she be replaced? Was this just a temporary stop for Rieve, like the last one?

The last one.

Her heart thumped.

It felt like it was in her throat.

What was happening? Why did she always feel so nervous?

It was just like when—

No.

The images came back:

The man in the dark cloak.

The alley.

The stormtroopers.

They were some of the last things she saw in Coronet City before fleeing and hiding on Nar Shaddaa.

On Nar Shaddaa . . . no.

The voice in her comms.

The parting of the crowd.

The explosion.

More flooded back, and it felt like the Ugyir River of Coronet City, overflowing its banks and flooding the city streets:

The burst.

The bodies flying.

The air ripped out of her lungs.

There were so many voices in her head then. Was it the crowd? She tried to focus on the podracers, but they weren't enough distraction from what was happening to her. It was like her body had traveled through time and taken her right back to those moments to relive them over and over again.

It would be only a matter of time before someone found out the truth.

Run.

No, she couldn't.

Run. Leave this place.

She had nowhere to go!

RUN.

She put her head in her hands and—

CRASH!

Rieve whipped her head up and saw the smoke, then the fire, then the podracer flipping over, colliding with the wall of the arena. A stout amphibian Urodel climbed from the wreckage and crawled to safety while the crowd went wild around Rieve.

Did you do that?

The thought, like the others, was sudden.

No, that was impossible. She had just been lost in her thoughts.

The crowd whooped and yelled as other podracers narrowly missed the fiery heap.

It was an accident. Just a regular accident, that was all.

But then someone looked her way.

Stared at her.

Then another.

They suspect you, the voice said. *RUN.*

Panic flooded Rieve's body. She pulled her hood tight over her head and stood nervously, her legs shaking. She made her way down the stands, toward the exit, and she heard someone behind her call out in Basic: "Hey! You!"

Rieve shouldn't have turned back. Her mind was a tangled mess, and one of Vespaara's closer suns sat perfectly above the edge of the arena seats, so she had to shield her eyes to see properly and—

No.

She saw him, just a flash. A tall man. A dark blue cloak.

Rieve nearly fell over, and when she looked back . . .

She couldn't make out who it was at that distance, but it was just a human male. No one special. Not *him.*

So she ran. Down the steps, through the concessions area, out the exit, and she kept running until she was safely inside her home.

Rieve pressed her back against the door and breathed deeply. She tried to calm down.

Maybe she'd imagined the man in the cloak, and maybe her paranoid mind concluded that she had caused the podracer to crash. It had to have been an accident, right?

But . . . so was what had happened in Coronet City, wasn't it? An accident. She hadn't intended for it to happen, and yet . . .

Rieve plopped down on her bed. Why did it always feel like horrible things followed her no matter where she went?

15

**ACK IN THE ARENA THE NEXT DAY,**
Rieve tried to push the events at the pod-
racing track out of her mind. So she was
deeply, deeply thankful that, as Dragus had promised, the
new Huttball battlefield—in the Gauntlet—was open and
ready for the first match of the season.

Balada had modeled it after a famous arena from the professional Huttball circuit, which pleased Grozz so much that
Rieve was pretty sure he was weeping into his fur before the
match. Rothwell helped Rieve stretch before disappearing
into the tunnel that led backstage, and she hopped from foot
to foot to keep her muscles warm.

She was on the Gundarks that day, alongside Grozz, Sentinel, and Imara Vex, and she couldn't be more pleased. They were going to *destroy* the other Hunters. It was a lot smaller in there than the other battlefields, so it seemed like the crowd was also closer to the action. She watched in anticipation as the pylons and traps were activated, as the stands filled with fans of every species imaginable and the noise in the battlefield rose and rose.

"You realize we've got the most famous Huttball player in perhaps the galaxy on our team, right?" said Sentinel.

"Well aware," said Rieve, smiling. "They don't have a chance."

"It's not just that," said Imara Vex. "We've also got another star here."

Rieve was confused at first. "What do you—"

Imara Vex shook her head. "Don't think I forgot about your little performance the other night. You're a celebrity."

Rieve dismissed it with a wave. "That was nothing."

"A celebrity?" said Sentinel. "What is she talking about, Rieve?"

Rieve didn't get to respond as the chime-bell rang out, and the four of them ran for the center, determined to get the Huttball before the Mudhorns. She pushed every thought out of her mind because she wasn't going to let herself be distracted by *anything*.

Unfortunately, J-3DI flung out his mechanical hand and reached the Huttball before anyone else. Rieve immediately activated her lightsaber, and the red blade sprang out.

"That's mine, Jedi!" she shouted, and she swung her blade in a low arc. J-3DI jumped up, which left him perfectly vulnerable to Grozz slamming into his body. It sent both the droid *and* the Huttball flying.

Rieve whooped in celebration, and Imara Vex immediately scooped up the Huttball. They charged to the other team's goal, where Slingshot waited, hoping to block any attempt to score.

He didn't see it coming. Imara Vex rushed in and faked out Slingshot at the last second, which caused him to leave the right side of the goal unguarded. Imara Vex quickly flung the Huttball to Rieve, who held it long enough to swing her arm back and toss it perfectly into the smaller upper goal for two points.

The crowd went completely wild; the Gundarks had scored in under a minute.

"I made that look *easy!*" Rieve cried out, and her teammates looked overjoyed at what they'd just pulled off.

She had begun to jog back toward the center of the playing field to prepare for the Mudhorns' advance when she saw him.

At first, she thought she'd imagined it, like she had in the podracing arena the day before. There, near one of the exits, was a tall man in a long cloak with a hood, the fabric a deep blue.

Rieve closed her eyes and shook her head, hoping she could make the image go away. It had to be her mind playing tricks on her.

But when she opened her eyes, he was still there, and he was no longer alone.

Four people, dressed in the brown combat uniforms she remembered from the alley in Coronet City, flanked the man in the dark cloak. Their faces were obscured by tight masks, their hands in black leather gloves.

It was the smugglers she'd met on that fateful night, and that had to be . . . *him*.

She had never seen his face. She had no idea what he looked like beneath the cloak. But that was *him*. And even though he was far from Rieve, he gave off a terrible, menacing energy.

"Rieve!"

Someone was calling her name. She couldn't tell who it was. She was focused on the man in the alley.

Or . . . the man in the stands.

Why did she feel so confused? Why was her heart racing so fast?

The man in the cloak turned and headed toward the exit in the stands, and Rieve knew then that she was afraid, just as afraid as she'd been in that alley when all those bodies went flying.

But this time, she wasn't trapped. Her back wasn't against a wall. He had come to *her*, and she had the advantage.

"Rieve, what are you doing?" Imara Vex stepped in front of her, blocking her view of the man in the cloak. "Get your head back in the game!"

"No," she muttered under her breath.

There was a new voice, this one in her comms. "Rieve, this is Rothwell," he said. "Is something wrong? Why are you just standing in the middle of the playing field? Do you need help?"

If she could have torn out her comms, she would have.

Instead, she *ran*, ignoring her teammates screaming after her, and she leapt up from the Gauntlet battlefield to grab onto the edge of the barrier. The crowd gasped as she pulled herself up and into the stands, where she landed in the lap of a surprised Aqualish.

The Aqualish glared at Rieve with their four eyes and then cursed her out in a language she didn't understand. But she kept moving, determined to make it to the exit and stop the man in the cloak. She balanced herself as she delicately sprang from one armrest to another. Some members of the audience swatted and hissed at her, while others cheered her on. She saw the back of the hooded cloak as the man began to walk down the stairs of the exit, and she screamed, "Don't move!"

A Wookiee stood up in front of Rieve, and she tumbled down.

She was quick to her feet, but the Wookiee shrieked at her. Rieve knew this was her fault, but the man in the cloak was escaping. "Out of my way, fur ball!" she screamed.

He howled back at her, his finger nearly in one of her eyes.

She tried pushing him aside, but he was strong, and her arms were exhausted from climbing into the stands. "Please, *move*! I'll have Dragus refund your ticket!"

Then the Wookiee shoved her.

She caught herself on a human female in luxurious silken robes, who cried out in horror. Rieve reared her arm back and was ready to strike the Wookiee, terrified that she'd just missed her chance to find the man who ruined her life, when she felt someone grab her shoulder.

She spun quickly and nearly punched Dragus in the face.

"That's *enough*," he said, his face twisted in anger. "The match is over."

And just like that, she snapped to the present. She looked around her at the horrified and bewildered faces of the people in the audience, then turned toward the exit.

The man in the dark cloak and his men were gone.

It hit her all at once: not only had the man from Rieve's past gotten away, but she might have just endangered her position as a Hunter.

"Okay," she said to Dragus. What else was there to say? When she looked him in the eyes, she saw confusion and pity there.

She let him escort her out of the stands and backstage as the memories flooded back in.

 **HE HAD BEEN SIXTEEN YEARS OLD** when it happened.

The package was like any other Rieve had been asked to deliver. Whatever it was, it was inside a small leather satchel, which fit easily within her pack. As was the custom for these sorts of jobs, she was given a time and a place. That was all.

Except this time, Feyr, her contact, told her to be careful.

"I don't normally do this, but you need to know," they said, sweeping their long black hair out of their face. "This is for the Rebellion."

She actually laughed at them. Feyr Jos'han, choosing a side. That wasn't possible!

"Wow," they said. "Laughing at me for making a choice? Maybe I'm tired of the occupation."

"Aren't we all?" Rieve said, taking the satchel.

"Please make sure this gets there," they said, and for the first time since Rieve had started working for them, Feyr seemed afraid. Sweat lined their brow, and they kept looking behind them.

"It will save lives," Feyr added.

"You say that every time," said Rieve, trying to make Feyr laugh.

But Feyr didn't laugh, and later Rieve would wish she had taken them more seriously.

She'd been working for Feyr for years at that point. With no family to depend on, Rieve had to rely on herself to get by. Feyr paid well, and they frequently needed her for deliveries of things that had to be kept under the radar. She was good at her job and was able to navigate the streets of Coronet City with an almost eerie sense of timing and awareness.

That night, Rieve would come to understand why that was.

It was supposed to be easy: a single drop-off point, just after sundown. As Rieve kept to the shadows and alleys, she wondered why Feyr was paying so much for such a simple assignment. The Empire was on its way out; she was sure of that. They couldn't occupy the city *forever*, and recent months had been full of news of defeat after defeat at the hands of the rebels. So what was the deal? What had Feyr spooked?

Maybe Rieve was just so used to being on edge that few things disturbed her anymore. Even when she sensed that she was being watched, it wasn't anything out of the ordinary while on the job. There were always thieves and assassins lurking in the dark. Coronet City was overflowing with them, especially after the Empire moved in. Imperial forces always seemed to bring out the worst in others.

Thus, it was business as usual. She was getting in trouble, like she always did. After she dropped off the package and got paid, she would wander around the city until she decided whether to spend the night on the streets or sneak back into the orphanage. Going back to the orphanage meant a clean, warm bed for the night, but she'd also earn another long lecture from one of the Togruta sisters, who disapproved of her "immature" behavior.

Her stomach growled. She could also try to get up early to get some breakfast before the Togruta noticed her. She decided that was her plan once she finished this job.

Until it wasn't her plan anymore. Rieve saw one of them, dressed in brown, lingering around a corner. He darted out of sight when she made eye contact. It didn't bother her; probably just someone looking to make a quick credit. It wasn't until the second one stepped out of another alley that she realized she was looking at uniforms, because the second guy was dressed identically to the first: brown utility vest over brown long-sleeve tunic, weapons hanging from a tight belt, black cargo pants falling on leather boots.

Okay, it's a coordinated effort, she thought, but it still didn't rattle her. There was no way they knew the backstreets of Coronet City like she did. She'd been running these streets since she was first able to.

So Rieve took off, and she had the nerve to laugh, because

what was there to be afraid of? She'd dealt with gangs and militias before, competing smuggler consortiums and petty thieves. These men were no different. She cut down one alley, sprinted to the end of it, then tucked herself around a corner, hiding behind a large stack of metal crates. By then, Rieve realized that there were far more than two of them. She watched as each one of the goons fell for it and continued running straight ahead. Her final count: *fourteen* people. As soon as they were past, she climbed up to the top of the crates, grabbed on to an overhang, and flipped herself on top of it.

"There she is!"

It didn't matter. She was already vaulting off balconies, running along rooftops, making it impossible for anyone to properly follow her. She crisscrossed to another building and howled with laughter when two of the men crashed into one of the ground-level mag-trains.

It was all natural to her. She didn't second-guess, she didn't have to plan anything out, and she never looked where she was going. It was like she could *feel* where she was supposed to step. Where she was supposed to land. Which alley was empty. Which street would loop back around and help her lose someone following her.

So Rieve didn't stop. The only sound was her own boots on the tiles. She bounded from one rooftop to another, sending a flock of starlows scattering. Their brown feathers sparkled in the streetlights, a reminder that their name came from how much they looked like starlight when they took flight.

She pushed herself harder. The shipyards were a few minutes away and—

Rieve sensed him just moments before his body plowed into hers, and once he hit her, she dropped, down, down, clipping her left elbow on something hard, something that sent a terrible jolt of pain up her arm. She hit the street below and couldn't breathe no matter how hard she tried.

Rieve looked up.

She was in an alley. One of them poked his head up over the edge of the building. How had he gotten up there? She was certain she had lost all of them. Gasping for air, she spun around on the ground to head away from the building, only to stare at the worst thing possible:

A dead end.

No, no! she thought, scrambling to her feet, ignoring the pain radiating up her side where she'd landed and from her left elbow. When she turned around in a panic, desperate to escape, they rushed toward her.

Five. Ten. Too many to count. All in those identical combat uniforms.

The closest one held a hand out. "Give it up," he said, his voice muffled by the formfitting mask he wore. She could see his eyes; he *looked* human. The man's hand, covered in a black glove, stretched closer and closer.

Rieve's lungs were burning, and terror raged in her chest. There was no escape from the alley, and even if there was, she still couldn't breathe.

She clutched at her chest with one hand. All the while, she backed up. Maybe there was a way out. Something she hadn't seen.

But there were no ledges or overhangs to leap up to. Nothing to grab on to, no way for her to launch herself up high enough to get over the wall that was now at her back.

They kept coming.

Rieve felt a buzzing along her skin. It rippled so fast that it raised goosebumps all over her body. What was happening? Was one of them using some sort of strange weapon on her? No, that wasn't it. She recognized it as what coursed through her veins whenever she tried to sense if someone was sneaking up on her. It was the same feeling she had when her intuition nagged her, telling her something was wrong or someone was lying.

They moved even closer.

There were so many of them. She couldn't take them on. She was too small. Too weak. Too young.

"There's nowhere to go," the lead man said. "Give us your package, and maybe we'll spare your life."

But Feyr had said . . . No. No, she couldn't hand it over. She didn't even really care about the Rebellion, but she *hated* what the Empire had done to the streets of her city.

"You leave me no choice," the man said, and he drew a blaster from his utility belt.

But he did have a choice, didn't he? She wasn't making him

do anything. He just wanted to feel better for what he was about to do: kill an innocent girl trying to complete her job.

Rieve stretched out her hand, palm out, and it was like time slowed to a thick, humid pace, and she could *see* his finger moving on the trigger and knew she had almost no time left before her life would end.

She thought a single word:

Away!

It built up so quickly that she couldn't stop it. All her fear and rage coursed outward, and as the man took another step, it *erupted* from her.

A wave of energy blasted outward, sending the men into the air, into the walls of the alley, into each other. At the same moment, the air was sucked out of her lungs all over again, and she nearly doubled over. Yet in an instant, it was over, and Rieve still held her hand out, stared at it in horror, heard the men groaning and crying, and she . . . she . . .

She had done this.

Rieve looked up. One of the men . . . he should not have been bent that way.

She had done this.

She allowed herself the briefest of moments to be shocked, to be overwhelmed.

You did this, a voice told her. *This is your power.*

She thought someone in the alley had said it to her, and it startled her. But there was no one else there. No one but the unconscious men scattered all about her.

Then she ran.

Rieve ran straight to the shipyards and was only one minute late. Her contact—a female Pantoran with bright blue skin who wanted Rieve to stay for a chat—muttered thanks as Rieve immediately made for home.

What have I done? she wondered.

But that thought was soon replaced with another:

How?

She knew it was risky to head to the orphanage because she might wake the Togruta sisters, but there was no way she was leaving Coronet City without what she'd hidden there.

At the orphanage, she slipped in through the back as quietly as she could. She snuck to the restrooms in the rear of the building, past shut doors and sleeping children, and she pressed her body against the cool floor once inside. There was a tile behind one of the sinks that could be pried off, and there she'd hidden all the credits she'd earned from Feyr and the audiochips she'd collected over the years. She stuffed them into a satchel, replaced the tile, and then promptly struck her head when she stood up.

The loud *thunk* echoed through the room, and moments later, Sister Xyla swung the door open. Rieve's face immediately sunk.

"Rieve, *really?*" she said. She was wearing a plain white robe tucked under her head tails that contrasted with the bright red skin of her face. "It's the middle of the night. Can't you just be a normal child?"

Rieve clutched her head. "I'm sorry," she said, and she was, because as she stood there, her life savings in a lone satchel, she knew she'd never see Sister Xyla again.

"You're always sorry, Rieve," said the Togruta, her voice low in disappointment. "I want you to be better."

Rieve was not a sentimental person, but she rushed forward

and put her arms around Sister Xyla. It was a quick thing, and she pushed her way around the Togruta. "I promise I won't bother you again!" she called out as she ran for the front entrance.

She slipped out as quietly as she could but immediately froze. Someone was coming toward the orphanage. Rieve ducked back inside, hidden behind the heavy fabric hangings that covered the entrance.

It wasn't some*one*. Rieve held her breath as an entire squadron of Imperial stormtroopers marched forward. Their boots echoed in unison.

What are they doing? she wondered, her heart thumping so loud she was sure they'd hear it.

The stormtroopers froze just two doors down from the orphanage.

"Which one, sir?"

He appeared from behind them. He wore a dark blue cloak that swept the ground as he walked, and his hood was so deep that she could not see inside it. She only heard his voice:

"Feyr said she was in the orphanage."

The voice was dark. Masculine. And it terrified her.

"But, sir," said one of the stormtroopers, "there are multiple orphanages on this block."

"Search them all," the man said. There was a terrible pause. "Bring her to me alive, so that I may have the pleasure of snuffing out her life. These children who think they can play in the lives of adults . . . They disgust me."

"Yes, sir."

The stormtroopers immediately split up, and the man in the dark cloak strode down the road. It looked like he was floating.

Rieve quietly backed away from the entrance, and then she escaped out the rear of the orphanage.

She didn't stop running until she made it to the galactic port. There she used a large chunk of her credits to book passage to the farthest planet from Corellia.

And Rieve never looked back.

○ ○ ● ● ● ○ ○

Weeks later, she was on Nar Shaddaa, a strangely familiar place. The moon orbited Nal Hutta in the Outer Rim, but on the surface Rieve found that, aside from there being less sunlight, it mostly looked like Coronet City.

Well, more like an exaggerated version of it. There was a densely packed cityscape over the entire moon, and Rieve found herself in Hutta Town, the capital city. Towers of metal loomed over everything, and she booked small lodgings in one of the skyslums, the encampments strung between the tower blocks. It was loud. Smelly. She was certain she inhaled every pollutant in the galaxy in that place. She met species she'd never even heard of before, let alone seen.

It was the perfect place to disappear from her past life.

She was a courier at first, which gave her some stability, and she proved herself to various smugglers and crime lords with her uncanny ability to avoid detection, despite not knowing anything about the mazelike streets of Hutta Town. It was in that city where she first heard of the Force, after one of her bosses made a joke about it. "I'd swear you had the Force," he told her after she had survived a dangerous job. "Except the Force isn't real, is it?"

That was how she was given the word to explain what

lived under her skin, what allowed her to sense the world around her.

And what sometimes made her a destructive force.

She met Yemar on one of those jobs a few years in. He'd been nothing more than a security guard for a local cartel she was trying to deliver to, something she'd laughed at when he told her. How did someone so tall and scrawny ever inspire terror or fear in *anyone*?

He'd laid her out on the ground just a few seconds later.

They struck up a fast friendship, especially once he shared that he'd been enjoying the local music scene. They compared audiochips and discovered they both loved a new form of music that had been born on Nar Shaddaa: gonkrock. Within the next year, they'd found Ully, a female Zabrak who loved the low-end instruments, and Boornan, a human woman who played a seven-string halllikset wired through a GNK power droid.

Corellia's Not Dead, they called themselves. It was Rieve's suggestion, a chance for her to remind the galaxy that her homeworld would always survive.

The band's reputation grew. They performed where they could and often where they *shouldn't*. Rieve lost count of how many gigs were shut down because her band simply didn't ask permission to play there. Corellia's Not Dead remained firmly underground, generating an obsessive following because of their legendary—and often violent—shows. They never really got out of the larger local venues, but bootleg audiochips of their shows spread across the galaxy. No one knew that during the day Rieve delivered contraband, weapons, and other items for local cartels and gangs. Because when Rieve stepped on that stage, she became someone else. All the anger and frustration she felt—over what had happened to her in Coronet City, over the scummy people she dealt with every day, over the constant nightmares she had about that alley— she found a release for in gonkrock.

They were headlining a gig at Yoshoyan's when it happened. It had been over five years since Rieve had left Coronet City, and the memory of what had happened there was clear only in her nightmares. The club was packed wall to wall, and before Corellia's Not Dead took the stage, all those bodies had raised the temperature inside by at least twenty degrees. It was hot. Sweaty. It felt like a war could break out at any time.

It was just the way Rieve liked it.

Their first song made it seem like a bomb had erupted in Yoshoyan's. Bodies flew about and crawled over the crowd. A young red-skinned Jablogian female screamed Rieve's lyrics back at her. Rieve herself was lost in the experience, as she always was, and she felt the energy that had been building up inside of her radiate away. This was her release. It was her *everything.*

In the rear of the club, a human male named Gortri was running the sound system, and a stranger—she never found out his name—grabbed the device that allowed Gortri to communicate with Rieve through a small commbud in her ear.

"This band is garbage!" he shrieked, and feedback squealed in her commbud.

Rieve crouched down and clutched her ear. She heard Yemar shout at her. "You okay, Rieve?"

"Get her off the stage!" the man cried out. "Pure garbage!"

Gortri's voice was much quieter. "Give me that back, you womp rat!"

"Who even *likes* this band?" the stranger screamed. "They disgust me."

She hadn't thought about those words outside of her dreams, but they rushed back all over again:

Images of the man in the dark blue cloak. The stormtroopers. The bodies flying.

Boornan tried to help Rieve up, but Rieve shoved her away.

No. No, it wasn't just a shove. Boornan stumbled, and Rieve realized too late that she had used the Force. What little training she'd given herself had focused only on how *not* to let it leak out of her. She could never repeat Coronet City again.

But it *was* happening again, wasn't it?

Boornan picked herself up as Ully rushed to her side. "What's going on, Rieve?" she asked.

She heard it in her comm again:

"THEY. DISGUST. ME."

And then . . . Rieve released the wave.

The crowd before her parted, screaming as she forced them aside, and then she had a clear view right back to the booth where Gortri was fighting off the man who had taken control of his comm system. She leapt forward. Gortri and the man were both staring at her as she approached.

The man pointed.

"Her!" he screamed. "She's the *worst* singer I've ever seen. You actually *pay* her?"

Those were the last words he said to her.

That was the last time she saw Ully and Boornan.

Her rage spilled out of her body in pulses of the Force, and she wanted to hurt this man, not even because he was rude but because he made her remember. The ceiling snapped, a long crack running from where Rieve stood and back toward the stage, and then there was a gigantic hole above her, made from the explosion of the Force exiting her body, and there were screams as pieces of the building plummeted to the floor and—

It was the crying that stopped her. She looked to her left,

and there was the young Jablogian, sobbing in terror at what Rieve had become.

Rieve did not know what that was.

She didn't look back at her bandmates. She ran. Straight to her home in the skyslums. And it was like that night in the orphanage again, except no one was chasing her as she entered the transport station in Hutta Town. Rieve had no idea where she was going next until she spotted the images of a Rodian and a Wookiee in combat on a holonet screen mounted above the waiting area. She watched it for a while.

Hunters. In an arena far, far from where she was now. It was too perfect, really. No one would know her there. She could disappear into an entirely new life.

So Rieve booked a one-way passage to Vespaara.

Because she could never go back.

**RAGUS DIDN'T SAY A WORD** until they stepped backstage. On the one hand, she appreciated not getting a public chewing out, but when she saw all her fellow Hunters awkwardly waiting around, she was filled with dread.

"You know, I thought it was pretty obvious," said Dragus, crossing his arms over his chest. "The audience? They're out of bounds. We don't go *into* the stands."

"I know," she said softly. "I'm sorry."

"I'm not sure 'sorry' is going to cut it, Rieve," he said. "What did you think you were doing? Were you actually going to *fight* a paying customer?"

"Did someone talk trash?" said Sentinel, walking up to

Dragus and Rieve. "I get it all the time. Some people don't like seeing the stormtrooper getup. But it's part of the entertainment, you know?"

"And you need to learn to *ignore* that," said Dragus. "You can't let them get in your head, Rieve. The fighting might be real, but the character . . ." He shook his head. "Don't get involved like that ever again."

For a moment, Rieve thought she had the perfect cover. She wasn't going to admit the truth to them. How would that sound? *Oh, some shady man from my past has come back to stalk me. Or maybe I'm imagining it. Or maybe the Force is making me think it's real! It could be any of the above.*

Rieve wasn't sure. The man had *seemed* real. But . . . had anyone else even seen him?

So this was it: she'd just let them all believe that someone in the crowd had gotten to her.

But then Imara Vex had to go and open her mouth.

"So, what was it?" she said. "What did they say to you?"

"It was nothing," said Rieve, immediately turning away from Imara Vex. "I'm sorry, Dragus, it won't happen again."

"Oh, come on," said Imara Vex. "Let us hear it. We'll tell you it's worrtwash. Because when you're off your game, Rieve, we're *all* affected."

"No," snapped Rieve, and she immediately knew she'd been too defensive. "No, it's not a big deal."

"Tell me what happened," said Dragus, stepping close. "*Now.*"

Rieve grimaced and tried to push down her rising fear. She decided to admit only part of the truth.

Rieve swallowed. "I thought I saw someone," she finally said. "Someone from Corellia. Someone who wanted me dead once."

There was an awkward silence, and Dragus cleared his throat. "And where did this person go?"

"I don't know," she said. "By the time you got to me, I'd lost track of them."

"Okay," said Dragus. "Okay, everyone, get out of here. There are no more matches left anyway."

The gathered crowd of Hunters shuffled away, all except J-3DI, who lingered nearby.

"If you could describe this person to me," said J-3DI, "I could perhaps scan the audience as they arrive next time and look for anyone who matches the description."

"No, no, that's okay," she said. "Thanks."

As J-3DI left her alone with Dragus, she felt relieved, if only for a moment. She couldn't have J-3DI looking for the man in the hood, too. How could she explain that she didn't actually know what he looked like? The whole story made her sound paranoid.

"I know this job is hard sometimes," said Dragus, his voice calmer than it was before. "But I need your head in the game, okay, Rieve?"

She nodded at him. "I know. I promise it won't happen again."

He raised a brow at her. "Okay. Go get cleaned up and get out of here."

She made to walk off, but then, behind Dragus, she saw Balada the Hutt slithering over to them both.

Dragus looked over his shoulder, then turned back to

Rieve. "Don't talk to Balada," he told Rieve. "Let me take care of her. I might run things down here, but this *is* her arena, so I'll smooth talk us out of this. I already have a spin: you were leaning too hard into your Sith Lord persona. Trust me, it'll work."

"Okay," she said. "I appreciate it."

"Go see your trainer. Make sure you're fine. And then I'll see you here tomorrow, okay?"

She didn't hesitate for a moment. She made straight for her prep pod, where Rothwell was waiting patiently. Rieve didn't even say hello to him. She just sat in the chair and stared up at the ceiling, letting Rothwell's scans wash over her.

Rothwell didn't speak. He went about his duties as if nothing had happened. He unwrapped her legs, gave her the red fruity drink that helped replenish her energy, and then worked on the muscle in her right arm that throbbed with pain.

Rieve had been so lost in her own head that she hadn't even noticed she'd hurt herself climbing into the stands.

"Make sure you get a good amount of sleep tonight,"

Rothwell finally said as he completed his examination. "My work can only do so much for you, Rieve. There's really nothing that beats some self-care and relaxation."

"Thank you," she uttered. "I'll try."

"There's a wonderful athlete's spa beyond the Employee District. Ask for Paola. Tell her I sent you. It might help you . . . relax."

Rieve nodded. There was a moment where Rothwell looked like he wanted to say something more. But then he smiled, shook his head, and left Rieve alone.

She stayed there for another hour in complete silence. She wished it all would go away: The stress. The fear. The presence of the man in the dark cloak. Why couldn't things just go well for her for once?

Before Dragus left the arena, he let Rieve know that his story worked on Balada the Hutt. "She ate it up, honestly," said Dragus. "She'll refund some tickets, but she believes that it'll actually bring in more sales. There's an 'air of danger' to the arena now. Her words."

"Oh," said Rieve. "Well, what a relief."

"I also need to tell you—and I quote—'Please tell that wermo that she can improvise as much as she likes, as long as she doesn't hurt my customers.'"

"That's . . . that's fair," Rieve said. "No more jumping into the audience."

"Get some rest," said Dragus. "Tomorrow is a new day, and you're killing it out there, Rieve."

She wished she could believe that.

Rieve left her pod only when most of the backstage area was quiet except for a few busy techs and cleaning staff. The fewer judgmental eyes on her, the better.

Because she still wasn't sure she belonged.

18

N HER BUNGALOW, Rieve couldn't sleep. She was ignoring messages from Zaina and Imara Vex, who wanted her to come out with them that night. She couldn't stomach that. They'd eventually lecture her on protocol and arena rules, and she didn't want to hear it. She knew she had messed up.

So Rieve left her home and began wandering.

She had no friends on Vespaara. Well, if you didn't count Dragus, but she wasn't sure if he was a friend or a mentor or neither.

It didn't matter. She hadn't been big on friends in Coronet City, nor did she become all that close to her bandmates on

Nar Shaddaa. (It still surprised her that Yemar had been so kind to her in the Oasis Cantina. Maybe he was saving his anger for later.)

At the orphanage, she'd known kids of all species, cultures, and genders, but she always kept them at arm's length. It helped that she was so odd and intense; no one seemed to want to be around her. Even her bandmates hadn't been sure where her lead singer persona ended and Rieve began. That was by design, of course. It was always easier to play a role than to be her true self.

But now?

Rieve felt invisible.

She ducked in and out of the crowds like a bay squid in the Ugyir River of Coronet City. (The squid had been killed off once the Empire set up shop on the banks of the Ugyir to construct Star Destroyers, dumping pollution into the once sparkling waters.) Just like that, whatever calmness she'd found in the silence of her prep pod was gone. She was antsy. Irritated.

Afraid.

Maybe she *had* imagined the man in the dark cloak. She'd been so stressed lately, obsessing over the past. What if this was a new way the Force had manifested in her life? That would be just her luck.

But . . .

But if that was really him, how had he found her?

Her feet took her to the only place she felt safe on Vespaara: the Oasis Cantina. A rowdy crowd stood outside the establishment, and it gave her hope. After the other night, she wanted to lose herself in some gonkrock.

It was just her luck, then, that when she asked the human male guard at the door what she could expect that night, he frowned.

"Our two local bands are off touring," he said. "We aren't quite the musical destination in this part of the galaxy, you know?"

"Blast it," she said. "Well, thanks anyway."

"If you're into other kinds of music, there's—"

She quieted him with a wave and turned to leave. There was no reason for her to stay.

And standing in the busy street, out of uniform and looking entirely out of place, was Rothwell.

He was scoping out the cantina, his eyes wide, his face a perfect portrait of the word *uncertain*.

Aw, he's out of his element! thought Rieve. *Finally, it's not only me who feels that way.*

Her night had just gotten a whole lot more interesting.

She called out Rothwell's name, and she was delighted by how relieved he looked when he saw her. He rushed to her side. "Hi!" he exclaimed. "It is very loud here! Why is it so loud? Am I shouting? Are *you* shouting?"

Rieve laughed—it felt like it had been weeks since she last laughed. "What are you doing here?"

"I don't know," he said. "It sounded pretty exciting down this street, so I just walked in this direction? That's all I got."

She pointed to the Oasis Cantina. "No offense, but I don't think that place is your scene," she said. "More my kinda thing, *especially* when there's music."

"Well, I'll let you get back to it," he said, and he started to leave.

"No, no, don't leave!" said Rieve. "There are no bands tonight. Just . . . walk with me."

Rothwell shrugged. "Sure," he said. "Where to?"

"I never have a location in mind. I just see where things take me."

They wandered together for a while, taking in the sights and people around them. It wasn't long before the two of them began inventing stories about whomever they passed. There was the Advozse, a thick-skinned female with a single horn on her head, selling trinkets from a cart, who Rieve said was surely in disguise and spying on a competitor. Rothwell made up the tale of the Abyssin female who had escaped the clutches of a terrible warlord she had angered and then traveled to Vespaara to go into hiding. By the time they looped around to the Huttball arena, Rieve had nearly forgotten the match from earlier that day.

Almost.

"Hey, so, I don't want to ruin the mood, but are you doing okay?" Rothwell asked.

Rieve shrugged. "I'm fine." She paused, then said: "I'm just worried I may have blown my chance today."

"I'm sorry."

"You have nothing to be sorry about," she said. "Doesn't have anything to do with you."

"I just mean that . . . well, whatever happened, it doesn't seem fair."

She groaned. "The worst part is that I'm not even sure I know what happened!"

Rothwell stopped walking. "What do you mean?"

"It's just that . . . I saw someone. Or maybe I didn't. But they reminded me of something from my past, and I just panicked."

"That's rough," said Rothwell. "Sometimes we don't like those reminders."

Rieve hesitated for a moment, then continued. "I'm like you," she said. "Something happened a long time ago, and I ran. I came here because . . . well, I guess I'm still running."

Rothwell was quiet. "I get that," he finally said. "I mean, I *really* get that. I think most of the people on this planet are escaping something. Why else would you come this far out in the Outer Rim?"

"I guess," said Rieve.

"Okay, let's assume this person you saw, whoever they are, is real. Then what?"

"What do you mean?" she asked.

"Do you think Dragus and Balada the Hutt can keep you safe from them? I'm not even sure I know what policies or protections are in place in case someone *does* decide to come for you."

"I don't know," she admitted. "I never really thought of it that way."

Rothwell started walking again, moving out of the way of a group of Rodian children whose parents were seemingly nowhere to be found. "I don't know if you can relate to this, but I always think about who I can trust at any given moment. Who do I feel safe with? Who's got my back?" He lowered his voice. "Who is going to blast me in the back?"

"Well, that's violent," said Rieve, wincing.

"You know what I mean," he said, smiling. "I just don't like putting all my trust in one person or even one job."

Rieve faked offense. "Are you telling me I'm not the only thing you deal with all day? The nerve!"

Rothwell laughed. "I split my time between Balada the Hutt's arena and some more underground stuff. Something that's not as in the public eye."

She narrowed her eyes at him. "Underground?"

"Some of the more obscure fighting rings," he explained. "I did tell you I had experience with that."

"Wow. I guess there's a lot more going on here than I realized."

"Well," he said, suddenly bashful, "if you ever need something else, or the whole Hunters thing doesn't work out . . ."

"Are you trying to *poach* me?"

Rothwell looked *horrified*. "No! Absolutely not!"

She cackled. "I'm playing with you."

He rolled his eyes. "Anyway. It's there. If you're looking for something else."

"Not now," she said, and then the two of them resumed their stranger story time as Rothwell walked her back to her house.

It wasn't lost on Rieve that she hadn't said no to his proposal.

19

IEVE WAS GLAD THAT SHE wouldn't have to deal with the closer crowd of a Huttball match. The day's task was simple enough: escort the payload through the Ewok Village on Endor. She just needed to focus, stick with the payload, and get past what had happened the day before.

She was placed on a team with Grozz, Imara Vex, and Zaina, who greeted her when she approached the tunnel backstage that led to the battlefields. "You get some rest?" asked Zaina.

Rieve gave a curt smile and nodded.

"We didn't hear from you last night," said Imara Vex, "but

you should come out with us sometime. I feel like you're open to getting in some trouble. And I *like* getting in trouble."

Zaina grunted. "You like starting fights."

"Isn't that the same thing?" said Imara Vex, grinning.

"Sure," said Rieve. "Sometime."

The four of them made their way down the tunnel beneath the arena, then cut right at the fork so they could head to the Ewok Village battlefield. Rieve didn't join in on the conversation the others were having. She worried that at the first opportunity, one of them would start grilling her on what had *actually* happened during the Huttball match.

The timer counted down.

You can do this, Rieve told herself. *Stick with the payload. Do that whole teamwork thing Dragus is always talking about.*

"You ready, Rieve?" said Zaina.

Imara Vex huffed. "She better be."

Rieve flashed a vicious smile. "I'm ready."

The timer hit zero, the chime-bell rang out, and Rieve and her team rushed forward to start the payload moving to its goal.

Grozz and Rieve immediately took the front of the payload, making it easier for them to engage any members of the opposite team as they approached. Utooni was their first victim as a blow from Grozz sent them spinning into Rieve's attack.

"Nice one!" Zaina called out, then fired beyond Rieve toward Sentinel.

Grozz pointed at his eyes with two fingers, then gestured in the direction of the tree line.

Someone was coming from that way. Rieve nodded, then turned back to make sure that Zaina or Imara Vex could provide her cover.

She saw him just beyond Zaina, back at the tunnel entrance to the Ewok Village:

A tall man in a dark cloak.

She froze. *No, Rieve, you're not seeing that,* she thought. She had to be imagining it. She jogged to Zaina, who glared at her.

"Rieve, get back to your position!" barked Zaina.

He was still there.

"Zaina, this is going to sound completely ridiculous," said Rieve. "But I need you to turn around."

"What?"

"Turn around!"

Bewilderment on her face, Zaina turned around slowly.

"Rieve."

"Yes?"

"Do you see someone standing there?"

Rieve felt a collision of terror and relief in her chest. "You see him, too?"

"Tall, dark cloak?"

Rieve wanted to cry. She wasn't imagining things!

Imara Vex had come to join them. "If you two don't stop fooling around and—" She froze. "Who is that?"

"So you see him, too?" said Zaina.

"Clear as day," said Imara Vex. She tapped something on the side of her Ubese helmet. "Normal heat signatures, too, so none of us are imagining this."

Finally, with a roar, Grozz came upon his three teammates, all locked in a staring contest with a stranger who had *somehow* gotten into their arena. He growled something at Imara Vex.

"I hear you, Grozz," she said. "How do you all feel about a little chase?"

Rieve smiled, thankful that for once she was not alone in her struggle. "Let's go."

The four Hunters abandoned the payload and chased after the tall man in the dark cloak, who turned and disappeared into the shadowed tunnel.

20

THE FOUR HUNTERS RAN through the team entrance and down into the tunnel beneath the arena, which led directly backstage. There were multiple voices chiming in over Rieve's comm, and she couldn't tell who they belonged to. Rothwell? Dragus? She knew she'd be in trouble after the previous day's interruption, but she *had* to find out who was following her.

Rieve pulled ahead. As soon as she crossed the threshold into the room, numerous techs, meds, and trainers gaped at her in shock and confusion.

"Where is he?" Rieve shouted. "Where did he go?"

No one answered her.

"We saw him," said Zaina, breathless as she came up behind

Rieve. "There was someone at the team entrance in a long dark cloak with a hood. How did he get in the arena?"

The tech closest to them, a Mon Calamari, shook her head. "I didn't notice anyone on the battlefield but the Hunters," she said, pointing to the giant screen in front of her. "Well, only four Hunters now."

Rieve looked frantically across the various feeds, pushing techs aside to get a better view. She saw the opposite team in the Ewok Village, pacing back and forth. They had to be pretty confused after their competition just ran away. The other battlefields were also empty, and the man in the cloak wasn't visible anywhere. She looked to both Grozz and Imara Vex, who shook their heads. They hadn't found anything.

"I *saw* him!" Rieve shouted.

Her voice boomed in the space, made even worse because of how quiet it otherwise was.

"Someone is trying to mess with me, and they were *here*. Where did they go?" She pointed to the team entrance tunnel she had just come through. "That only exits into this room, so he has to be here!"

Rieve heard footsteps approaching, and she watched as Dragus ran up to her. "Rieve, what is going *on*? Why aren't you in the arena?"

Rieve made to say something, but Zaina stepped in front of her. "Dragus, she's not lying. I saw him, too." She paused. "Or I saw *something*. A person in a dark cloak, standing at the team entrance."

"What?" Dragus looked around the room. "But . . . there's no one here like that."

"I saw them, too," said Imara Vex.

"You too?" said Dragus. "Are *any* of my fighters on the field right now?"

Grozz warbled something.

"But this place is under the highest scrutiny!" Dragus walked closer to the massive row of surveillance screens. "We see everything!"

The Mon Calamari grunted. "Well, people *have* been coming and going from that entrance constantly. Trainers, meds, droids . . . there's a constant stream into this place. So, it *is* possible that someone slipped by us."

It built quickly. There was no warning. Rieve had been relieved that someone else had seen what she did, but that feeling was gone. The rage grew in her chest and spread outward, and soon there was no way to control what was happening to her.

"Where is he?" she screamed. "That's not possible. It's not possible!"

She rushed to the nearest prep pod and hit the door control, only to find Charr—the Trandoshan Hunter—busy trying to get dressed. He snarled at her. "Some privacy, please!"

Rieve closed the door. Opened another one. And another. And another.

"Rieve, what is it?"

She spun to see Rothwell approaching, his arms out, palms facing her.

"Rieve, is there anything I can help with? I tried to reach you over comms. What's going on?"

Rothwell couldn't help her. No one could.

She smashed her fist into the door of the next prep pod, and when it buckled, she realized she had a new audience.

Sentinel. Utooni. Dizzy. J-3DI. The match must have been stopped because . . . well, who were they supposed to compete against?

They looked so confused. Scared. Bewildered.

Even J-3DI, who wasn't a living being, seemed afraid.

Rieve turned back to the next prep pod. She was convinced that the man from her past was hiding in one of them. Her anger swirled, and the voice pushed her. *Do it,* it told her. *Destroy it all.* And she wanted to! She wanted to tear the place apart until she found him.

And then what?

Rieve didn't have an answer.

Dragus finally intervened. "Stop it, Rieve!" he begged. "Stop!"

"But he's *here!*" She turned to face Dragus. "What are you going to do to protect me? Do you even believe me at all?"

Dragus was so close to her, and his face was twisted up in worry. He reached out and put his hands on her arms. "Please, Rieve, just calm down. Let's talk about this."

"I'm done talking about this!"

And with those words came the release.

Rieve could no longer control what was building up within her. When she pushed her arms outward to break contact with Dragus, the Force surged through her.

Dragus flew backward, skidding across the floor. There were gasps, along with the sound of Dragus's breath being knocked out of him.

Regret swirled through her, but it was overshadowed by everything else.

Fear. Anger. Rejection.

"I can't do this anymore," she said. "If it's not one thing, it's another!"

She was methodical in removing her arena gear, placing it on the chair next to her lightsaber. As she stripped off the med tape, Rothwell came closer. "Here, let me help you, Rieve," he said softly.

She spun around and glared at him.

"Hear you loud and clear," he said, his hands up. "I'm around if you need me."

Then he was gone. She felt a wetness on her cheeks. When

had she started crying? Rieve wiped at the tears, and then Zaina was there, holding out a small towel. Rieve grabbed it to dry her face.

"Cry it out," said Zaina. "You don't need to hold it in."

The man in the cloak was there. She knew that with all her heart. He was tormenting her. Maybe he'd come to finish the job he'd started on Corellia.

"I'm not safe," she said quietly, and the truth of that swept through her. She wasn't safe there. She would probably need to leave Vespaara, too.

For now, though, she couldn't be in the arena anymore.

She grabbed her outfit and stuffed it in her bag but left her lightsaber behind.

"Not safe?" said Zaina. "What do you mean by that?"

With her knapsack over her shoulder, Rieve charged through backstage, trying her best to ignore all the pitiful looks everyone was giving her.

"Please," said Zaina, chasing after her. "I believe you, Rieve."

Rieve stopped for a moment.

"So do I," said Imara Vex. "I saw him, too."

Then Rieve shook her head.

"But he doesn't," she said, pointing to Dragus, who was being attended by someone from the med team.

"That's not true!" Dragus called out, and as he tried to get up, the med tech pushed him back down. "Rieve, I—"

Rieve didn't let him finish. She left everyone and everything behind as she ran for the arena exit.

HE WAITED.

There was a large crowd outside the arena. There were daily tours of the various arenas, all promising insider views of the competitive sports and the athletes.

Like everything else there, it disgusted him.

He didn't have to wait long. She came rushing out of the entrance that Hunters and staff members used, and she looked . . .

Upset.

Which meant that it wasn't going to be much longer.

It had gone exactly to plan.

21

 **T WAS HAPPENING ALL OVER AGAIN.**
Rieve knew her time in the arena was over. She was sure of it. There was no way Dragus would ever let her go back, not after what she'd done. She didn't need some fancy Jedi teacher or Sith Lord to tell her what she knew about herself: sometimes everything became too overwhelming, and she couldn't control the Force within her.

It would happen again. And again. And again.

And with the man in the cloak trying to find Rieve? It would absolutely happen if he caught her.

Rieve considered packing up her few belongings and running to the Vespaara Transit Hub, but the idea of that was also too overwhelming at the moment. *Do other people feel like this?* she wondered. *Do they doubt themselves this much? Do they have a dark voice in their head that tells them the worst about themselves? How do others seem so comfortable when I don't?*

Rieve was convinced she was the only person who felt the way she did.

She wondered if the man in the cloak knew where she lived. *That* thought made her more nervous, so she left her home and made for the only logical place. Yet even when she stood outside of the Oasis Cantina, she couldn't bring herself to go inside. She had enjoyed playing gonkrock on Nar Shaddaa, but that had been just an escape, hadn't it? That wasn't who she really was.

Who *was* she?

A fighter? A Hunter? How could she figure out who she was when all she had was torn away from her so often?

The Force prickled along the edges of her consciousness. It was always there, mostly in the background, but in moments like this, it came to the front of her mind. It was supposed to be some sort of mystical connection with everything living in the galaxy. But what good did it do her? The advantages it gave her paled in comparison with the moments when it backfired. What good was the Force to someone like her?

Rieve sensed him first, so she wasn't surprised when Rothwell's head poked out above a passing crowd. There was a moment when she thought he was going to continue on without noticing her, but he turned his head at the last second.

"Rieve?" he said, then jogged over to her.

It was still odd to see him out of his normal trainer uniform. He had on a loose-fitting black tunic over tight purple pants and street boots. He looked . . .

Normal.

"Hey," she said as he came up to her. "Where you headed?"

"Doesn't matter. How are *you*?"

She waved the question away. "You wanna find somewhere else to go?"

He frowned at her. "No, I'm not going to be that easy to get rid of, Rieve. Seriously, what's going on with you?"

"Not you, too," she groaned. "Everyone is so concerned about me, but no one wants to—"

"I believe you."

She heard the echo of Zaina's and Imara Vex's words in Rothwell's. She *was* glad that they'd seen the truth, and if things hadn't turned out like they did, she could even imagine herself becoming friends with them.

But with Rothwell . . . she didn't understand why. It just meant more that he'd said it.

"Thank you," she said, her voice low. "I don't know what to do anymore."

"For what it's worth, we all looked," he said.

"What? What do you mean?"

"Everyone looked through *every* part of that arena. Every bathroom, every prep pod, all the parts of engineering that none of us normally go to . . . We tried. We never found anything."

Rieve sighed. *Great,* she thought. *Even if I wanted to go back, he's still out there.*

"Jay-Three even scanned the place," Rothwell continued. Then he put on his best imitation of the droid: " 'My sensors have come back inconclusive. May the Force be on or around you!'"

She laughed hard at that. "Seriously, did Sprocket purposely program him to talk that way?"

"I mean, *I* would," said Rothwell. "Just to annoy other people."

She wondered then if she was annoying to the rest of her teammates.

The prickle along her skin came back. Rieve had no idea what to do, and even worse, without the arena as an outlet, she had nowhere to release the energy building within her. She wasn't close to an explosion—not like she'd been backstage, in that alley on Corellia, or on Nar Shaddaa. It was only a matter of time, though. How long could she hold it in?

Wait.

There was a place she could go.

Rothwell was the answer.

At least a temporary one, she realized. "You told me something last night," she said.

"Oh, no," he said. "I am not to be held accountable for *anything* I said last night."

She laughed. "No, it's good. You told me that if I ever needed something else . . ."

Rothwell's eyes went wide. "Oh! *That*."

"Yes, *that*."

"But . . . does that mean you're quitting the arena?"

"I don't know yet," said Rieve. "But in the meantime, I don't want what I did to Dragus to happen again. I need to release the energy in me or . . . well, you saw what happened."

He grimaced. "Okay, fair enough."

"Well, let's go," she said. "I didn't have any matches today, so I'm ready."

Rothwell hesitated. "Oh, I don't know if that's a good idea."

"Why not? Are you *afraid* of me?"

"What? No! It's just . . ." He frowned. "I can't just bring in *anyone*. At least not without vetting them through my boss. It's an underground ring for a reason. There aren't a lot of laws here on Vespaara, but we still gotta keep everything under the radar."

She sighed. "Yeah, that makes sense," she said. "But how long do you think it will take?"

"Well, how about this? Meet me in the Warehouse District tomorrow. Say . . . midday?"

"Ugh, who knows what time is anymore on this planet?" she said.

"I *know*," said Rothwell, grinning. "It's an awful adjustment, isn't it?"

He gave her directions. "I'll introduce you to the guy I work for," he said, "and you can watch a few fights, then maybe give it a go?"

"Maybe," she said. "*If* they're up to my standards."

He laughed. "Perfect."

Rothwell turned to go, but Rieve reached out and grabbed his arm.

"Thank you," she said.

He nodded. "Given everything that's happened, I think this is the best decision for you right now."

Rothwell walked away, and she hoped he was right.

22

*HE NEXT DAY* Rothwell greeted Rieve by immediately making fun of her.

"Rieve, are you wearing your Hunter gear?" he asked as she approached their meeting spot. "Do you sleep in it? You probably sleep in it."

"No!" She ran her hands down the front of it. "I've actually never taken it home with me before."

"You're not worried about people recognizing you?" he asked as they started walking.

Ah, right. That was one of Balada's rules: no fighting in any other arena or organization.

"I'll figure something out if there's a second time," she said. "Plus . . . it's *really* comfortable."

"You're weird," he said. "But that's what makes you so fun."

Rieve had never traveled to this side of the boomtown on Vespaara. There was no need for her to do so; it was the industrial area, where all the production warehouses and factories were. Most of the buildings were long and flat, save for the occasional smokestack or exhaust pipe. Some of the buildings smelled of Vespaaran rock candy, another popular treat in the arenas; others had a bitter, toxic scent. Rothwell was narrating their journey, explaining what each factory made for the growing industry on the planet.

She wasn't paying attention, though. A new wave of nerves rattled her. She had no idea what she was stepping into, and her Force sensitivity felt rawer than usual. She could sense almost every living being in the buildings she passed. So as they got closer and closer to their final destination, Rieve was ready to burst.

I really hope this works out, she thought.

Because she was terribly eager for a fight.

The eternal twilight cast long shadows on the largely unfinished road, and Rothwell pointed to a flat, plain gray building at the end of it. "That's it," he said. "I know it doesn't look like much, but that's sort of the point."

As if on cue, a Gamorrean—green skin, wide snout, horns jutting from his lower jaw and the top of his head—rolled out of the entrance and across the ground, then lay still. The sound of shouting, clapping, and braying poured from inside the building.

"What the—" she began.

"A perfect introduction," said Rothwell, clapping her on the back. Then he guided her forward and, stepping right over the motionless Gamorrean, took her to the front door. A human woman with a shaved head nodded at Rothwell but then scowled at Rieve. "She's with me," he said.

"Of course, sir," she said, then stepped aside.

"Oooh," said Rieve, teasing Rothwell. "Well, of *course*, sir. Your *majestic* presence is very impressive, Rothwell."

"Shut up," he said. "The people here just know how to respect others, that's all."

Once Rieve stepped inside, she struggled to adapt to what she was seeing. It was *chaos*. While the room stretched out before her in seemingly every direction, every part of it was occupied by someone or something. Every part except for the small ring at the center, where a female Gran had her six-fingered hands raised above her head in victory.

"Wow," said Rieve in Rothwell's ear. "You weren't kidding."

She watched as ingots passed hands, often coupled with rude comments and loud protests, or credit chips were scanned for bets. A short Hassk stepped into the makeshift ring next, and a voice rang out in Basic over the gathered crowd:

"BETS MUST BE PLACED IN THE NEXT MINUTE. NO BETS ALLOWED AFTER THE BELL RINGS."

It repeated in various languages, and Rieve wasn't sure how *anyone* focused on anything in this place. There were so many voices and sounds overlapping one another. She didn't even know what she should be looking at! She noticed that a few of the beings in the crowd were glancing over at Rothwell and her, then nodding their heads.

"Does everyone know you here?" she asked.

"Mostly," he said. "I'm the main medical point person, so

when people are severely injured—which happens more often than not—I jump in to assist."

They moved deeper into the crowd, and then Rothwell tapped her on the shoulder. He pointed to the other side of the room. "See that Peezee protocol droid over there?"

Sure enough, tucked behind a Trandoshan and a dark-skinned human female wearing long elaborate braids over a patterned robe was a bright blue protocol droid.

"That's Peezee-Eighteebee," Rothwell continued. "We just call her Eighteebee for short. She's sort of the . . . referee? Well, she's that *and* kind of like your announcers. Plus a translation unit."

"All of that?" said Rieve. "How?"

"You can get your comms linked to Eighteebee," he explained. "She will translate everything for you. She's pretty spectacular, actually. Can run something like five hundred processes at once."

Rieve watched as PZ-80B raised one of her short mechanical arms and her voice boomed across the warehouse. "BETS ARE PLACED," she said.

A bell rang.

The fight *erupted*.

Despite how short the Hassk was compared with the Gran, he was *fast*. His gray face stood out against the dark fur of the rest of his body, and Rieve had to admit he looked intimidating. He darted around the Gran, then between her legs, punching her in the rear of one. She held it and howled, then stomped down toward the Hassk.

Rieve realized how much more *brutal* this fight was than what she was used to in the arena. She gasped along with the audience, and Rothwell laughed.

"A bit different, isn't it?" he said loudly in her ear. "Not that the arena isn't dangerous, but this?" He smiled. "There's nothing like it."

Moments later, the fight was over, and the Hassk stood victoriously over the Gran's unconscious form. It was a major upset, and judging by the reaction from the crowd, most had bet on the Gran winning.

"You wanna try?" said Rothwell.

"Don't you need to help her?" she asked.

He shook his head. "Her sponsors have her," he said, then gestured with his head.

Sure enough, the Trandoshan that Rieve had seen earlier had pulled the Gran up from under her arms.

"So, as I said," said Rothwell, "you wanna give that a try?"

Rieve's mouth dropped open. "Me? Do that? *Now*?" She shook her head. "I mean, I *want* to. Aren't you supposed to introduce me to your boss first?"

"In time," he says. "Promise."

"Shouldn't I start a little smaller? Maybe some training rounds or something?"

He scoffed at her. "There is no training here, Rieve. This isn't a professional arena. It's just . . . fighting. You volunteer, people place bets, and anyone who wins gets a cut of the night's earnings from the entrance fees."

"Which means," said Rieve, "the more you fight and win . . ."

"The more money you can make," finished Rothwell.

"Smart system," she said. "Gives you more incentive to fight better."

"Exactly," he said. "I get that there's definitely a competitive edge as a Hunter, but . . ." He shrugged. "This just feels more real, Rieve, and I think you could honestly make a killing here."

It *was* what she wanted. Something brutal and efficient that would allow her to expend all her pent-up emotions. Maybe this was it. Even if she still kept the Hunters gig, this could be her main focus when she wasn't in the arena. It would be a delicate balance, though, as Hunters were forbidden from participating in any other fighting competitions—official or not.

She watched another fight, a vicious one-on-one between the Gran, who wanted another chance, and a human male who somehow matched the Gran's two meters of height. The two of them danced around each other in a hectic back-and-forth, each of them taking and giving hits that seemed to sing out in the warehouse. Soon Rieve realized she was bracing herself before the fighters got hit, as if she was in the ring herself.

It called to her. She had to do this.

"You know what?" she said, cracking her knuckles. "I'm young. I'm strong. Why not?"

Rothwell could not have smiled wider if he tried. "That's exactly what I want to hear," he said. After the match ended—with the human standing over the Gran's unconscious form—Rothwell whistled and waved at PZ-80B. She rushed to his side, and there was a hushed conversation before the droid looked at Rieve.

"Her?" she said. "*She* wants to fight?"

"Thanks for the vote of confidence," Rieve called out.

"I vouch for her, Eighteebee," said Rothwell. "I wouldn't bring just *anyone* here, right?"

PZ-80B examined her. "You ever fought before?"

"I fight in Balada the Hutt's arena almost every day," said Rieve.

PZ-80B scoffed at her as much as a PZ protocol droid *could* scoff. "Trash. That's not fighting. It's choreographed nonsense."

Rieve frowned but didn't take the bait. What happened in the arena was anything *but* choreographed. "Put me in a fight. I'll show you what I can do."

The droid looked to Rothwell, who nodded.

"She knows she isn't supposed to be here?" she said to Rothwell.

"I know," said Rieve.

"And she knows that there are no training gloves here?"

Rieve snapped in PZ-80B's face. "I'm here," she said. "Talk to me."

"Okay," said the droid, and if a droid could be smug, this one was. "Next fight. You won't know your opponent until you're in the ring."

"Fair," said Rieve.

"You fight until one of you is out."

"Understood."

"And you're going to get hurt," said PZ-80B. "Expect it."

Rieve smiled. "I can handle it," she said. "Nothing like a little violence to calm the nerves."

The droid tilted her head to the side, and Rieve could tell that if she was able to roll her eyes, she would. "Save the edginess for the fight."

Rieve's heart raced as PZ-80B left her with Rothwell.

"Rothwell, am I really doing this?" she said, practically bouncing in place.

"You're doing this."

"*Should* I do this?"

He laughed. "You absolutely should."

The crowd parted, and Rieve had a direct path to the ring. She gave Rothwell one last look—"Go, go!" he shouted—and then made her decision.

RIEVE VERY QUICKLY REALIZED that she might be in over her head.

Standing across from her was her opponent, a towering Iktotchi male, two horns on the sides of his wrinkled head twisting downward to his chin. He was hunched over, his hands out in front of him, his shoulders dancing side to side, ready to pounce on Rieve.

Bets had been placed. She was certain that *no one* had bet on her. She wasn't in her Sith Lord face makeup, she was missing parts of her costume, and she definitely did not have her lightsaber. So to these people? She had to be a complete nobody, just some foolish girl who volunteered to have her butt kicked.

The bell was going to ring any minute.

Well, she thought. *Time to prove yourself.*

The bell echoed through the warehouse.

And Rieve didn't even have time to react before the Iktotchi tackled her.

She hit the ground hard, but not hard enough to knock the air out of her. She struggled for a moment, then wrapped her legs around the Iktotchi's torso. Rieve squeezed, then rolled over until he slammed against the ground.

He cried out, and she untangled herself and rose. The roar from the audience was practically deafening as she did so, and it was even harder to block it out there than it was in the arena. Everyone was so *close* to her!

Focus, focus, she told herself.

The Iktotchi rose and dusted off his long robes. He swore at her, or at least that was what the barked words sounded like: a curse on her very soul.

Well, bring it, she thought. She was ready.

He charged.

She saw him leading with his right hand.

And Dragus's training popped into her head: *A fighter will reveal a lot about themselves if you just pay attention.*

Rieve stood her ground, right until the Iktotchi was about to nab her, and then she leapt out, grabbed his right arm, and flipped him over her shoulder.

The sound of him hitting the hard ground?

Oh, it was *so* satisfying.

All that pent-up energy . . . was gone. It had evaporated. She turned to the massive crowd and raised her hands up, pumping them in the air, screaming along with them.

And *that* was when something hit her in the back.

She didn't know what it was at first. There was a sharp pain along her shoulder blades, and she remembered in that instant that she was not wearing Balada's mysterious med tape wrapped around her body. Clearly that stuff worked, as a burning pain spread across her back.

But it didn't stop Rieve. She spun, gasping for air, and saw the broken remains of a wooden crate on the ground.

"Where did you even *get* that?" she screamed. "Are we allowed to use *crates*?"

The Iktotchi merely spat on the ground in front of her.

"Oh, so you want to play dirty then?" she said, goading him on. "Let's play dirty."

She had seen no weapons in the ring during the fights she'd witnessed, so she understood this was all hand-to-hand combat. Except . . . a crate wasn't a hand *or* an appendage. So was the Force off limits?

Rieve waved the Iktotchi toward her, all the while concentrating on him, feeling his micro movements, sensing which side he was going to charge from.

She'd never really entered this heightened state in the arena. There were too many distractions, too many chances for her to get lost in her own thoughts. Somehow, this felt *more* pure. She was taken back to her time on the streets of Coronet City, always sensing whether there was someone lurking around a corner or in the shadows.

The Iktotchi flinched, trying to fake her out.

That wasn't going to happen.

He swung at her, hard and fast, and she perfectly moved out of the way so he would clip her right shoulder. It gave him enough of a sense of victory that he dropped his guard. He went for an uppercut with his left hand, and like most fighters, he forgot that he had legs.

Rieve looped her left leg behind his and shoved.

He went sprawling on the floor but was quick getting to his feet.

Not quick enough, she thought.

Her foot connected with his chin, and even she was impressed at how far his body flew. The Iktotchi collided with the onlookers on the opposite side of the ring, and even though they tried to hold him up, it was clear that with a single kick Rieve had knocked him clean out.

The noise that overwhelmed Rieve filled her with pride. People were screaming at her, shock and joy on their faces, and she'd never felt anything like it. It was as if an electric current ran through her body, and she screamed back at them as she paraded around the ring.

"VICTORY TO THE NEWCOMER!" announced PZ-80B. "PAY UP, LOSERS!"

As Rieve watched credits changing hands, the epiphany

came all at once: she *was* a good fighter outside the rules and regulations of the arena! Maybe Rothwell was right. Maybe Dragus and Balada the Hutt had been holding her back this entire time.

Because there, on her own, without structure, Rieve *thrived*.

She turned around and scanned the crowd, a smile filling her entire face. Where was Rothwell? She wanted to celebrate with him; he was, after all, the entire reason she was there. Plus, how much had she just earned? Rothwell had mentioned that each winner got a cut of the credits.

"Rothwell!" she called out. "Rothwell, where are you? I wanna go again!"

At the sound of Rothwell's name, the crowd hushed. It was immediate and unnatural, and the hair on Rieve's arms rose. One moment before, the space had been chaos.

And now . . . it was order.

No, that wasn't right.

She looked at the faces in the crowd.

No.

They were *afraid*.

Directly across from her, the audience of gamblers and spectators parted, like they had earlier for Rieve, like . . . oh, no. The image was there in her head again: the crowd on Nar Shaddaa.

It wasn't happening again, was it?

The gathered onlookers moved slowly, and then *he* was there, sauntering toward her, his dark cloak nearly dragging on the ground, and the most terrible panic erupted in her body, sent the Force flowing through her. And she was furious, so furious with Rothwell for bringing her there. He knew, didn't he? He knew exactly who Rieve had seen in the arena, and he was working for him, and this was all—

The man in the dark cloak lowered his hood.

Rieve stared into the delighted face of Rothwell.

**R**OTHWELL LAUGHED.

"You know, I didn't even think I was gonna have time to go change," he said, striding forward. "You beat your opponent so quickly! Bravo, Rieve. I shouldn't have underestimated you for a second."

"No," she said. "No. What are you doing? Why are you dressed like *him*? How do you even know about—"

Rothwell waved a hand. "Tonight's event is over," he said loudly. "Leave."

With no hesitation and without a single word spoken, the majority of the gathered crowd shuffled out of the warehouse. But some remained: The now-conscious Iktotchi. The Gran.

The Gamorrean. At least forty others, all of them muscular, terrifying.

Fighters. Rothwell's fighters.

"I'm not dressed *like* him," said Rothwell. Then he smiled again in a way that didn't reach his eyes. "I *am* him."

"Th-that's im-impossible," she stuttered.

"Is it?" he said, and she noticed that those who stayed behind had formed a ring around her. Rothwell circled Rieve slowly. "Did you ever see my face back on Corellia? Because I went to great lengths so that no one knew what I looked like."

"No," she said softly. "No, this isn't happening."

"It's clear I know who you are, and I know what you did, Rieve." He paused, then stepped close so his face was only a breath away. "I know what happened in that alley."

She backed up, right into the Hassk from earlier, who shoved her forward.

"This doesn't make sense!" she blurted out. "What are you doing? Why?"

"Because YOU TOOK EVERYTHING FROM ME!"

He yelled so hard that his spit landed on her face.

"I had a *business* on Corellia, Rieve! I was successful! And then *you* came along, and you had something I needed and—"

"That package?" she said, her face twisting in confusion. "Why?"

"Do you realize how important medical supplies were at that point in the war, you *fool*?" Rothwell raged. "You had antiviral medications. Vaccines. Vials of kavam and alazhi."

She shook her head. "Rothwell, I don't know what that—"

"Bacta!" he screamed. "The *best* healing solution in the entire galaxy!"

"Who cares?" she shot back. "Can't you get that anywhere?"

He lashed out and grabbed Rieve by the collar. "You have no idea what you set in motion with your little *display*," he sneered.

She shoved him away from her, but he came right back, his face in hers.

"*I* was supposed to deliver those precious supplies to my Imperial contact in the shipyard. Imagine my surprise when I found out that Feyr Jos'han had what I needed. Feyr wasn't supposed to get that satchel. *I was.* A wrong delivery; that's all it took. Someone gave them *my* supplies by accident, and they sold them."

Rieve remembered how panicked Feyr had been.

It will save lives, they had told her.

Feyr had tried to warn her, and she hadn't listened.

Rothwell continued to circle her. "And so I tried to give you a chance, once my men found you. All you had to do was give back what was mine."

"It was just medical supplies," she said as confidently as she could, despite the fact that she was terrified.

"You don't get it," said Rothwell. "Coronet City was *mine.* I worked hard to control as much of the trade in that city as possible."

"I don't care!" she yelled.

"But I do! Because when I came up empty-handed after you reduced my couriers and guards to a blubbering mess, guess what happened? My Imperial contact accused me of selling out to the rebels."

"*What?*" she said.

"It doesn't matter that it wasn't true, because once the Empire convinces itself of a narrative, there's no *un*-convincing it, Rieve."

He grabbed her again. "They locked me up. Me, and everyone who ever worked for me. Sent some of us off to labor camps. I lost *everything*. And to what?"

Rieve looked behind her.

There was nothing but a solid line of Rothwell's fighters.

"I thought you were part of another cartel or gang," he said. "That you had some bizarre power, that you were trying to prove yourself by taking out my people. I mean, what an egotistical, selfish, useless way to live! I thought no one cared about you, so you had to make your big, splashy debut by destroying someone's livelihood."

His lip curled in a snarl.

"By destroying someone's *family*."

Rieve's mind was racing. *No!* she thought. *That's not what I did at all!*

Rothwell shoved her to the ground. "After the Empire fell,

we were rescued," he said as she struggled to get upright. "Set free. I went back to Coronet City, but by then, everything I'd done there meant nothing. There was no work."

He knelt next to Rieve. "I lost it all, Rieve. Everything. Contacts. Money. My reputation."

"That all sounds like something the Empire did, Rothwell," she said, digging her elbows into the ground. She pushed herself up so she was in *his* face. "It's not my fault you couldn't run a business."

For a moment, it looked like Rothwell was going to strike her. But he smiled again—that awful, soul-crushing smile of his, not the one she'd seen when Rothwell was being friendly to her backstage or outside the Oasis Cantina.

"You're not in a position to insult me, Rieve," he said.

She knew she wasn't, but insulting him was the only response she had to all the epiphanies rushing through her.

How much of the past couple of weeks had been fake? *All* of it?

Details came back. Things Rothwell had said about his past. Like how he'd had to run because something went wrong.

His determination to learn how to survive. The odd jobs he'd picked up along the way.

The underground fighting ring he worked for.

Rothwell had found a way to lie to Rieve by telling the truth.

"I rebuilt what I lost," he continued. "What you *stole*. It took years, Rieve, and you were long, long gone."

His fighters stepped closer.

"And then I found you. Or, rather, your *owners* told me about you."

Rieve crawled away from him. "What? Why would they—"

The ad. The ad Balada had sent out, telling the galaxy that she had a real-life Sith Lord in her arena.

"I see you figured it out," he said, his voice softer. "One of my couriers never forgot your face. Do you know how easy it was to apply to be your trainer? It wasn't like people were begging to assist a *nobody*."

Rothwell reached out and brushed her white hair out of her face. "No one thought twice about telling me anything I wanted," he said. "Who you were. What little they knew of you. I told Dragus that I wanted to be the best trainer possible, and he gave up everything he knew. I could follow you anywhere, and do whatever I wanted, and no one questioned me."

"It was you," she said. "In the stands. At the team entrance."

"Oh, Rieve, think a little bit deeper than that!" he exclaimed, standing up. "You think that's all I did?"

One of his fighters—the Gran—stepped up to Rothwell and handed him a long curved blade. "Rieve, I thought you were a match for me."

"What does *that* mean?" she choked out.

"You took out how many of my people?" He seemed to float over to Rieve. "You ruined their minds. You destroyed my whole life. And then I came here, expecting to find a true adversary, someone who was worth all this strife and struggle and pain. You know what I found instead?"

Rothwell crouched again, and the blade got closer and closer.

"A nobody."

He rested the curved edge on her throat.

"A scared, insecure, pathetic *loner.*"

He pressed it into her skin.

"You're still trying to prove yourself to others. You're still without friends, without a family, without *anyone* who cares about you."

Rothwell snickered.

"Manipulating you . . . even *that* was too easy. You're so desperate to be liked."

She hated him. She hated everything that came out of his mouth.

And she hated that he might be right.

"You're a disappointment," he said calmly as he stood and took a few steps from her. "I thought sabotaging you would be fun, Rieve. I wanted to watch you squirm. I wanted to see you reveal yourself as the powerful villain you think yourself to be."

He smirked.

"But you're nothing."

Rothwell unfastened his cloak and let it fall to the floor.

"I'm tired of wearing that," he said. "It is *way* too hot here! Besides, I don't have time for you anymore, Rieve. I've wasted years of my life on *nothing*. I have an arena to destroy."

"What?"

Rieve tried to get up, but as soon as she got to her knees, the Gamorrean sucker punched her in the head. She saw stars swirling in her vision as she struggled upright again.

"Did you think I was going to stand here and reveal my plan to you and *then* give you a chance to escape?" Rothwell laughed again. "No, dear. Not in the slightest. I wanted to ruin your life like you ruined mine, but then I got here and I realized that not only are you a worthless life-form, but there is just so much *money* to be made. I can make back what you stole from me . . . tenfold. Twentyfold. The nebula sky is the limit here on Vespaara."

Rothwell's fighters closed in.

"So I'm going to sabotage your arena one last time."

Sabotage. Like everything else he'd done to her: The faulty lightsaber. The malfunctioning ACU. What else? Had he hired the Rodian in the Huttball arena? Who in her life was part of Rothwell's plan?

Would she ever know the truth?

"Because when Balada the Hutt's arena is gone, the people here will still want to see fighting. They'll just get to see the *better* form of it. No med tape, no trainers, no bacta tanks . . . the real thing."

He laughed. "You've seen what I can do here with my fighting ring. You know how much more real it is firsthand. And you now know that in the end no one cares about your silly personas or stories. They just want *blood*."

Rieve finally pushed herself up, her head still ringing from the Gamorrean's punch.

"I am going to take everything from you, just like you did from me," Rothwell said.

"I'd like to see you try," Rieve said, hoping it sounded convincing. But she knew it didn't. Her head ached, her skin buzzed, and Rothwell's fighters were almost within arm's reach.

"Have a lovely day, Rieve," said Rothwell, waving to her. "Since it's your last."

Then he cackled. "Wow, I've always wanted to say something like that!"

He turned.

The circle of fighters grew even smaller.

His voice echoed over them all.

"Get her."

**HIS WAS A DISASTER.**

It was obvious to Rieve that none of them knew who should make the first move, and maybe that was because they all saw how quickly she had dispatched the Iktotchi. For a moment, she used that to her advantage.

She lunged at them.

Some of them flinched away.

"Are you afraid?" she said. "Don't know what to do without Rothwell?"

Unfortunately, she was also vocalizing what that voice in her head was telling her, the one she'd started hearing after that fateful day in the alley.

You have no idea what you're doing, it told her. *You know they're going to destroy you.*

She swung on the Hassk and missed.

But you don't know your own power, it said. *You have no idea what you possess.*

She ducked to avoid a punch from the Gamorrean.

Take them all out.

She breathed in deep.

All of them.

Exhaled.

They deserve it.

Maybe. Maybe they were all just as awful as they seemed in that moment. But Rieve couldn't. She couldn't unleash the Force, because if she did, the cycle would start all over again. She would hurt others in a moment of panic. She would run away. She would find somewhere new. And it would begin once more.

Everything Rothwell had told her would be true.

As Rieve stayed light on her feet, as she dodged and swerved out of the way, she realized just how tired she was of running.

Of having to find new places to live, new ways to survive, new people to disappoint when she inevitably left.

The voice urged her to attack, its tone desperate and pleading, and she wished her thoughts didn't sound that way. She couldn't control them, and having Force sensitivity on top of it?

"NO!" she screamed.

The energy thrummed along her skin.

The Gran rushed her.

She raised a palm and the Gran *froze*.

There was a collective gasp from the fighters, and Rieve wasted no time. She flung the Gran aside, and her body crashed into the wall of the warehouse.

And just like that, the fight was truly on.

The Gamorrean charged her next, and she stopped his fist with an open palm. As she squeezed it—and his eyes went wide—she struck out with the toe of her boot, nailing him in his shin. No sooner had he gone down than another fighter tackled her. She struggled to stay upright as the Hassk pounded on her side, all while she tried to keep the Force contained inside of her. If she let it go at this point, she couldn't possibly guess what would happen.

What if it was *worse* than what had happened in that alley in Coronet City?

She growled and then body-slammed the Hassk into the ground.

Someone pulled at one of Rieve's legs as the Hassk wheezed under her. She kicked out, but then someone *else* had her by her left hand. She grunted, trying to pull them down with her, but to her surprise, the Iktotchi—very much not unconscious anymore—*sat* on her hand.

"Get her down!" someone cried out, and then there was no controlling what she felt anymore. The fighters squeezed in, holding down all her appendages, and the Gamorrean laughed.

"Did you really think you could take on all of us?" the Iktotchi said. "None of your silly Sith magic matters."

"I am not a Sith!" she screamed.

It surged.

It was right at the surface.

The silhouette of the Iktotchi, with his twin horns, hovered over Rieve.

"I'm going to enjoy this," he said.

He raised his foot in the air.

A blast rang out, and Rieve was ready to let go, ready to lay waste to all of them, ready to run away once more.

The Iktotchi pitched to the side.

"What?" she said.

There was a commotion, and Rieve twisted her head up, looked right where the Gran had been.

At the end of the warehouse, her blaster raised in the air, Zaina whistled.

"Who's ready for a *real* fight?" she said.

**HEY POURED IN BEHIND ZAINA:** her teammates.

There were Sentinel, Imara Vex, Dizzy in his droideka, Grozz howling with his droid arm weapons in the air, and Utooni, with J-3DI bringing up the rear and wielding his bright blue lightsaber.

Rieve had never been so happy to see J-3DI.

The distraction was all she needed. She felt a burst of hope, and it was enough to allow her to focus. For the first time, she actually felt like she had the Force under control.

It lasted only a few seconds, but that was long enough.

With a scream of rage, Rieve lashed out, but she held some of her power back. The fighters around her stumbled

back—just a meter, if that—and for a moment, she was pleased with herself.

She had controlled the Force.

She had controlled *herself.*

Rieve flipped off her back to stand upright, and the fight raged around her. She saw Imara Vex slam one of Rothwell's fighters into the ground—with one hand, no less.

"Got you!" Imara Vex screamed as she stood over the groaning Gamorrean.

Then she paused and studied the fighter's face. She pulled a bounty puck out of a pocket and activated it.

"Seriously?" said Rieve. "Right *now?*"

"A job is a job," said Imara Vex, and she slammed some cuffbands around the Gamorrean's wrists. "I wonder if there are others. . . ."

Rieve was going to say something, but a howl of rage rang out. She saw the Gran she'd fought earlier charging her.

"Oh, no you don't!" Rieve said, and she blocked two of the Gran's punches before swinging an elbow into her jaw. The Gran yelped in pain, and Rieve spun around, sensing that the Hassk was about to jump on her back. She kicked her leg out, and down the Hassk went, howling the whole way.

"Rieve!"

She swiveled her head in the direction of the voice and saw Sentinel struggling with two Trandoshans. She sprinted toward him, then slid the rest of the way so she took one of the Trandoshans down.

"Thanks!" said Sentinel, and then promptly knocked out the other one.

It was chaos. Zaina's blaster had been kicked out of her hand, but Rieve smiled when she saw Zaina beat down the human male who had celebrated disarming her too early. Grozz . . . Grozz seemed to be having the time of his life, growling with joy as he pounded down one fighter after another. Even Utooni and Dizzy, who had paired up to literally run circles around a group of Duros, seemed to be thrilled to let loose.

And then J-3DI called out Rieve's name.

She turned to see the droid toss something in her direction, and by the time it landed in her palm, she was ecstatic.

The red blade of her lightsaber lit the face of the terrified Moldwarp male before her.

"No thanks," he said, then turned and ran.

Rieve spun about. Blocked blaster fire from someone who had picked up Zaina's blaster. Got said blaster back with minimal bloodshed. She sensed someone coming up behind her and—

Imara Vex put one of her hands up. "I'm on your team, remember?"

In the other hand, Imara Vex was dragging the limp form of the Iktotchi.

"I thought Zaina shot him!" said Rieve.

"Oh, she did," said Imara Vex, and she fished out *another* bounty puck, which contained the holographic image of the sleeping Gran. "Two for one! Not a bad haul."

Rieve laughed and looked around. In just a few short minutes, the entire warehouse was filled with groaning, moaning, wheezing, or unconscious fighters.

"Not bad," said Rieve. "Do you guys fight for a living or something?"

Zaina stepped forward with her arms outstretched, then stopped. "You know, I was gonna go in for a reunion hug," she said. "But I realized I don't even know if you *like* hugs."

"I don't," said Rieve, but she held out a hand. "But I'm glad to see all of you."

The two shook hands briefly, and then J-3DI was quick to ruin the moment.

"Rieve!" he blurted out. "We are so thrilled to have found you. Our Sith Lord has returned to the fold!"

"Wait," said Rieve. "How *did* you find me?"

They all pointed at J-3DI in unison.

"Wow," said Rieve. "I mean . . . thanks, Jay-Three."

"It was no problem. The Force guided me to you."

She tilted her head to the side. "You don't . . . you don't have to do that here," she said.

"Do what?" he said.

"We're not in the arena," said Sentinel. "You don't have to pretend."

"But I'm not," he insisted. "I'm a Jedi Knight. The Force guided me here."

"Let's move on," said Rieve, shaking her head in confusion, "because we have a bigger problem on our hands."

"Move on *where*?" asked Dizzy.

"To the arena!" said Rieve. "We have to go back there."

No one spoke. Zaina looked at the floor, and Grozz kicked a furry foot into the side of one of the fighters, who was still out cold.

It took Rieve a moment. "Oh," she said. "Right. I . . . I kinda bailed on the arena."

"You didn't need to leave," said Zaina. "You didn't even give us a chance."

"It's not that we didn't believe you," said Sentinel. "But everything had *just* happened, and you foolishly were convinced no one was on your side."

"What was I supposed to do?" said Rieve. "I don't know any of you very well."

"Then let us *try*," said Zaina. "Imara Vex and I attempted to."

"And I don't try with almost *anyone*," said Imara Vex. "If you're not a Hunter or a bounty, I don't care."

"In our own way, we're family," said Zaina.

"Who else is gonna have our backs?" said Dizzy. "We're a bunch of weirdos way out in the Outer Rim, beating each other up for the entertainment of others. If we don't have family out here, then what *do* we have?"

"A lot of bruises," mumbled Imara Vex.

Family.

But . . . but they weren't her family. She'd never had one. How could Zaina throw that word around so carelessly?

"I don't know about that," said Rieve. "I've never had a family."

"Zaina's not wrong," said Imara Vex. "Did you think that just because you're a jerk sometimes, you're not part of this family?"

"Why do you keep saying that?" said Rieve. "I'm not related to *any* of you."

"While the word *family* has literal definitions across the galaxy," said J-3DI, "there are many possible permutations upon which to arrange a family, including those with whom you share no genetic—"

"Not quite the right time to spew out definitions," said

Dizzy, stepping off his droideka and facing Rieve. "But he's right."

"I don't get it," she said.

"Do you know how many people shunned me on my homeworld?" said Dizzy. "Or thought I was a fool for picking up that old droideka and restoring it? I brought her and myself to Vespaara, and not *once* have my fellow Hunters made me feel like I don't belong."

"We may not belong elsewhere," said Sentinel. "I certainly don't have many places I could go. But I belong *here*."

"We don't care where you came from or what happened in the past," said Imara Vex. "We just care what you do *now*."

Grozz howled in agreement while the Jawa twins chirped excitedly.

Which was right when one of the fighters next to Grozz groaned loudly. He put a furry foot over the fighter's mouth.

"Look, I'd love to stand around and talk about our feelings," Rieve said, "but we need to get back to the arena."

The Jawa twins that made up Utooni chirped up a storm. Rieve didn't speak Jawaese, so she turned to J-3DI.

"They said that you really don't have to fight tonight," he translated.

"Yeah, we'll all take the night off with you," said Zaina. "Let the other roster double up."

"No, no, that's not it," said Rieve. "My trainer—Rothwell—he's on his way to sabotage the arena!"

"Rothwell?" Imara Vex frowned. "The guy that looks like the underside of Grozz's foot?"

Grozz warbled in protest.

"Sorry," said Imara Vex. "You want me to apologize to your foot?"

"What are you talking about?" asked Zaina. "What did Rothwell do?"

"We don't have time," said Rieve, giving the warehouse one last look. "I'll tell you on the way!"

They sped out of the building, but not before Rieve kicked the Iktotchi as hard as she could.

"One last round for good measure," she said.

It made her feel a little bit better, but not enough.

How was she going to stop Rothwell?

 **TOONI STOLE A SPEEDER FOR THEM.**
Rieve was a little shocked. They were standing outside of the warehouse, arguing with one another about the fastest route back to the arena. Sentinel wondered if maybe a couple of them could hop on Dizzy's droideka, but Dizzy said he would declare war on the first person who touched his beloved transport. Grozz, on the other hand, had told J-3DI that he could beat him in a foot-race, and J-3DI was ready to accept the challenge, which was when Utooni pulled up in a speeder.

One of the Jawa twins chirped at J-3DI.

"Oh," said the droid. "Seems we were so occupied with our

little . . . disagreements that our lovely Jawa friends took it upon themselves to procure some transportation."

Rieve wasn't sure, but when the Jawas said something back to J-3DI, it kind of sounded like an insult.

So they all piled into the speeder, and Dizzy kept pace alongside them in his droideka. They zipped through side streets, and Rieve hoped they'd reach the arena in time.

In time for *what*, though? What did Rothwell mean when he said he would sabotage the arena?

"So," said Zaina. "We've got some time. You gonna tell us what's going on?"

Crammed into the back of that speeder, still processing everything Rothwell had told her, Rieve decided to take a risk and tell the truth.

She started talking.

She told them about being an orphan on Corellia. About all the jobs she used to do, how good she got at avoiding detection when she ran packages for Feyr, how she was cornered in an alley by Rothwell's men.

How she had exploded and learned she was Force-sensitive,

and how that changed her whole life. She told them about her time on Nar Shaddaa, the mistake she'd made, and what brought her to Vespaara.

"You had no one to teach you what the Force was," said J-3DI from the back of the speeder. "So it is understandable that you were confused by its appearance and alarmed by what you could suddenly do. The Force chooses to manifest differently in each person. I, for one, see the Force as binary code."

"But you don't *actually* have access to the Force," said Sentinel.

"I'm a Jedi Knight," said J-3DI matter-of-factly. "We must be Force-sensitive in order to be trained."

While the others argued about J-3DI, Rieve began to piece something together herself. What if that voice inside her head was how the Force communicated to her?

"Jay-Three," she said, interrupting the argument. "In all that Force lore you've got, is there anything about *how* the Force can appear in a person? Could it . . . could it be a voice?"

The speeder turned a corner sharply, and one of the Jawas throttled the engine.

"It is entirely possible," said J-3DI. "Some people experience the Force as a feeling. As music. As gentle rainfall on their spirit. It is unique, and it is likely that you've known exactly how yours manifests for a long time."

"Then why is my voice so negative?" she said to herself, promptly forgetting how good J-3DI's hearing was.

"Because your internal voice can be affected by countless other factors," he said. He paused, then said, as sincerely as possible: "It sounds like you've been through a lot, Rieve. Everything you just told us about your life on Corellia and Nar Shaddaa . . . it is indeed possible that your internal voice could match that of the Force. Maybe your voice is a reflection of what you have experienced. And maybe that's your own mind trying to protect itself."

Rieve wished that they weren't pressed for time, that they weren't racing to stop their arena from being destroyed, because for the first time since she'd met him, Rieve wanted to sit down with J-3DI and have a conversation.

Instead, she told the others about Rothwell.

"So he's the one who's been messing with you this whole

time?" said Sentinel once she finished. "Wow, that's . . . that's really creepy. I would like to have a few words with him."

"By 'words,' you mean 'fists,' right?" said Imara Vex.

"Oh, you know me so well," said Sentinel.

"That makes me feel gross," said Zaina. "Like . . . like I need to take forty showers just to get rid of it."

"Well, whatever you feel, it's worse for me," said Rieve. "And now he says he wants to 'sabotage' the arena. And I have no idea what that means!"

"You realize that as your trainer," said Imara Vex, "Rothwell has access to the *entire* arena."

"That's a good point," said Sentinel. "We have no idea what secrets he knows."

"Or ways to take arena operations offline," added J-3DI.

"Wonderful," said Rieve. "So we're still just as clueless as we were ten minutes ago."

"We're almost there," said Zaina. "We'll figure it out."

"In the meantime," said Imara Vex, "I need to hear a *lot* more about you being in a band. You never told us anything else after we saw your little performance!"

"I heard you were quite the Troithe sewer rat onstage," said Sentinel.

Rieve gasped. "You *told* him?"

"What?" said Imara Vex. "You thought I was going to keep that a secret? You got a lot to learn about this family, Rieve. *Everything* is fair game."

Despite the kindness from her fellow Hunters, Rieve was all nerves by the time Balada the Hutt's arena came into view. She hopped out of the speeder only to see Dragus come rushing out of the arena's main entrance.

"I am so glad to see you all," he said, nearly out of breath. "The arena needs your help!"

 **EFORE DRAGUS COULD EXPLAIN,** though, he locked eyes with Rieve.

"Oh," he said. "I didn't expect to see you again."

Shame rippled through her. "I'm sorry, Dragus," she said. "I shouldn't have hurt you."

He frowned. "You think throwing me across a room is all it takes to hurt me?" He waved a dismissal at her and smiled. "What kind of fighter do you think I am?"

"Still," she said, smiling back. "I need to apologize to you."

"Later?"

Rieve nodded. "Later."

"Good," said Dragus, "because we've got a bigger problem to deal with."

The sounds of the crowd in the arena echoed in the background.

"Please tell me the other Hunters aren't competing right now," said Imara Vex. "Are we too late?"

"Too late?" exclaimed Dragus. "Too late for what? I haven't even told you what's going on yet!"

"Oh, we already know," said Sentinel. "Lemme guess: something about sabotage?"

"A bunch of extremely oversized goons are trying to fight everyone?" offered Imara Vex.

"Yes," said Dragus, his face twisted up in confusion. "How on Vespaara do you know that already?"

"Technically," said Rieve, reluctance in her voice, "it's kind of my fault?"

"No, no, we will not be doing that!" said Imara Vex. "Some creep deciding to play out a completely misguided revenge plot on you is *not* your fault, Rieve."

"Could *anyone* actually tell me what you are all talking

about?" screamed Dragus. "My arena is probably being torn apart at this very moment!"

"It's *Rothwell*," Rieve seethed. When Dragus looked at her, confused, she continued. "My trainer?"

"I know who he is," said Dragus. "I was the one who hired him."

"Well, he's messed up pretty much everything," said Zaina. "And we're here to stop him."

"I've got some fists that are *aching* for a fight," said Sentinel.

"So . . . *he* is the one responsible for all the strangers in the arena?" said Dragus. "I don't know who they are or how they got in, but they're ruining everything! Sprocket is injured, Tuya got knocked out, and I don't know what's going on. They're planting charges, destroying the battlefields. . . . It's *chaos*."

"He's the man in the cloak," explained Rieve. "The one I saw in the stands. He's been sabotaging me ever since I started fighting."

"Wait," said Dragus. "So you mean . . . the broken ACU. The one you thought was part of a prank."

"Yep."

"Your broken lightsaber."

Rieve nodded.

"That time you ran into the stands . . ."

"All of it," said Rieve. The more she thought about it, the worse her anger got. And the angrier she became . . .

She needed a release. *Badly.*

"But why?" Dragus said. "And what does this have to do with the arena?"

"Dragus, we don't have time to revisit Rieve's childhood through a bunch of poignant flashbacks," snapped Zaina. "What do you need us to do?"

"Get in the arena," he said. "Last I heard before I came to find you, our cameras caught some of Rothwell's people in the other battlefields. Get them out!"

Dragus started to run off.

"Where are you going?" said Rieve.

He turned back briefly. "I have my own way to help," he called out. "Go! Save our arena!"

As he left, the Hunters stared at one another.

"We have to find Rothwell," said Rieve.

"And we've got to get rid of a bunch of invaders," said Sentinel.

"We have no idea how many of them there are," said Dizzy, hopping back in his droideka.

"Who knows what this Rothwell is planning?" said Imara Vex.

Grozz howled.

"So . . . we don't have a plan," said Rieve.

"Nope," said Sentinel. "Except me punching people."

"That's a good enough plan for me," said Imara Vex, a mischievous smile spreading across her face.

The eight Hunters ran into the arena through the front gate, then ascended the stairs, rushed past concessions, and sprinted out into the stands. The first battlefield on this end of the arena was the Ewok Village, which wasn't currently in play.

Which was why it filled Rieve with dread to see a group of Rothwell's fighters scaling the *other* side of the battlefield.

She pointed at them. "There! What's beyond this place?"

"It's the Outpost on Tatooine," said J-3DI. "We can cut through the tunnel underneath to reach it faster."

Rieve extended her lightsaber in the direction of the invaders. "Let's get them," she said.

R *IEVE HAD NEVER SEEN THE ARENA* in such a state.

Her roster mates spread out in the Tatooine Outpost. Since it was a smaller battlefield and had a vaguely circular shape, Imara Vex volunteered to get to a high point to act as a scout. Rieve held her lightsaber in a defensive pose at the entrance to the Outpost as the Hunters began to engage with Rothwell's fighters.

Skora, the Rodian healer, rushed up to her. "Rieve, right?" she said. "What's happening? Who are these people?"

"It's an invasion," she said. "Dragus sent us in to help."

"Perfect," said Skora. She loaded more darts into her gun. "So just . . . take out as many of these goons as possible?"

"Exactly," said Rieve. "Tell your teammates that this isn't part of the show!"

"So I get to *actually* do some damage?" said Skora. Rieve could hear glee in her voice. "This is the best day of my life!"

As Skora ran off, Rieve had only a moment to take stock of what was happening before a high-pitched, ear-splitting alarm rang out with three sharp bursts.

"What is that?" Rieve screamed.

A monotone voice echoed through the arena: "PLEASE DO NOT BE ALARMED. FOLLOW SIGNS TO THE NEAREST EMERGENCY EXIT."

The alarm rang out again, and Rieve pressed her palms over her ears. The message repeated in various languages, and Rieve wondered what her best move would be. Find Rothwell? Help her teammates? Locate Balada the Hutt? What if Balada was up in her ship, which still hovered over the arena?

Standing there indecisively wasn't helping at all, though, so Rieve finally ran into the Outpost. *Might as well do some fighting!*

Which was when all the power went out.

If it weren't for the eternal twilight of Vespaara, the arena would have been completely blanketed in darkness. As it was, the shadows left behind in the blackout were eerie, and suddenly Rieve could no longer see anything properly. She sheathed her lightsaber.

Great! she thought. Was this part of the sabotage? What was Rothwell planning? How could she do this on her own?

Then she remembered Rothwell making fun of her just hours before. *Do you sleep in it? You probably sleep in it.*

She was still in her arena gear! And that meant—

"Anyone who is listening," she whispered into her collar, "what's happening?"

Please let this work, please let this work.

"Rieve!"

She heard the voice in her comms first, and then there was motion nearby.

She saw J-3DI's glowing blue lightsaber before she saw the droid. "Put that away!" she whispered harshly as he approached her.

"Oh, right," said J-3DI. "The glowing blade announces my presence."

"What's happening? Why did the power go out?"

"If I were to guess," he said, "I would assume that Rothwell is responsible for this. He is trying to make it harder for us to stop whatever he has planned."

"That little creep," she said. "Jay-Three, can you head beneath the arena to see if you can fix this?"

"An excellent idea, Rieve," he said. "History will not forget this day, when a Jedi Knight and a Sith Lord worked together!"

She didn't even bother correcting him. Instead, Rieve snuck over to the lighting fixture where Imara Vex was. Imara Vex quietly slid down and joined her.

"I can see Grozz over there," said Rieve, waving to him. "Where did all of Rothwell's fighters go?"

"I can see heat signatures in the adjacent battlefield," said Imara Vex, "but I can't tell if they're Hunters or the fighters."

Rieve decided to take a risk. "Any Hunters, to me!" she screamed, then ignited her lightsaber.

There was movement in the Outpost, and then the Hunters

began to appear: Grozz. Sentinel. Utooni. Zaina, Aran Tal, and Diago Velaar, a Miraluka sharpshooter Rieve didn't really know. He wore a stylistic gray band over his face, and Rieve remembered that was because his species didn't have eyes. Diago was a legend in the arena because he used his hearing to locate the other Hunters.

"Where are the rest of the Hunters?" asked Rieve.

"They've moved into the Aftermath battlefield," said Aran. "I sent them after the invaders. What's going on? Where's Dragus?"

"I don't know where he is," said Rieve, "but we need to get these fighters out and find my trainer, Rothwell." She didn't say her next thought aloud: *How am I going to do that?*

"At least the audience is leaving," said Sentinel.

"Jay-Three is trying to get the power back on," said Rieve.

"What are we supposed to do?" said Zaina. "I barely remember what Rothwell looks like."

"I can try to find a better vantage point to take out some of the invaders," said Diago. "Just call out to me so I know not to shoot you."

"Perfect," said Rieve. "Go!"

As Diago ran off, Rieve's mind raced. She was doing her best to quell the panic in her, because nothing would be less helpful right now than an uncontrolled burst of the Force.

"What do I do, what do I do?" she repeated aloud.

"Let us help you," said Dizzy. "We are family. Like Zaina said. And family *helps*."

Dizzy wasn't wrong, but Rieve felt completely out of her depth. She was used to running, not staying and fighting.

Leave, then, the voice said. *You can use the Force to disappear undetected. Leave them all behind. You don't deserve them.*

"Shut *up*!" she screamed. "I'm so sick of you telling me what to do!"

There was silence—not just from the voice in her head, but from the other Hunters.

"Sorry," she said. "Long story involving the Force."

"Rieve, this is Jay-Threedeeaye. Come in, Rieve."

Rieve grabbed at the collar of her costume. "Yes, this is Rieve. Tell me you're fixing the power."

"I am doing my best, but so far I've only been able to

activate the power for the central core and backstage. I'm still working on it."

The idea came to her suddenly. "Thank you, Jay-Three. You have no idea how helpful that is."

"So, what's the move?" asked Sentinel.

"We're doing this wrong." She smiled and grabbed Zaina by the arms. "Teamwork."

Zaina looked confused. "Sure. Yes. Teamwork is good!"

"What are you saying, Rieve?" asked Imara Vex. "We don't have time for mysterious riddles!"

"Dragus has been trying to get me to reconsider how I fight, and he's always saying that I act impulsively and without consideration for my teammates."

Imara Vex cleared her throat. "Oh, don't mind me," she said when Rieve glared at her. "Just agreeing, that's all."

Rieve held in a sarcastic retort and pushed on. "All of you know this arena better than me because I'm the newest Hunter. So let me be your eyes and ears. Your lookout! I can go backstage and tell each of you where Rothwell's goons are."

There was another distant explosion.

"It's a great idea," said Zaina, "so go. Tell us through our comms! Grozz, come with me!"

Zaina and her group headed toward the sound of the explosion, while the others split up to cover other battlefields. Rieve headed back to the team entrance in the Outpost. Even in the near darkness, it was easy to find because there was a slight glow coming from somewhere deep inside the tunnel.

She passed some unconscious fighters.

Not bad, she thought. *J-3DI must have taken care of them.*

When she made it backstage, she ran just a few meters into the room. She discovered the source of the glow she'd seen from the tunnel: the power was definitely back on! Perfect.

The room was in a terrible disarray. Chairs were strewn everywhere. Some of the prep pods were smoking, and there was a large crack across one of the screens at the center of the room. She didn't see any techs, meds, or trainers, let alone J-3DI.

She did see some more unconscious fighters on the floor.

Who were they? Was she too late?

Before she could turn her head, she felt a warm blaster pistol against the back of her neck.

 **IEVE SWALLOWED HARD.**

Why? Why had she let her guard down? She held her deactivated lightsaber out in front of her.

"See?" she said, waving the lightsaber. "Whoever you are, you're in control."

The person holding the blaster said nothing. Rieve tried to twist her head to the left, hoping to see who was behind her, but the pistol was pressed harder into her neck.

"Sorry," she said. "Tell me what you want."

"Rieve?"

J-3DI's timing was either impeccable or a nightmare, and

Rieve wasn't sure which. But the droid stood across the room, staring at her.

"I might need some help," said Rieve, tilting her head toward whoever held her hostage.

"Why does Balada the Hutt have a blaster to your head?" he said.

"What?"

She spun quickly, and sure enough, somehow Balada had slithered up behind Rieve while she had been surveying the room. Balada muttered something in Huttese.

"She says she thought you were an intruder," said J-3DI.

Balada rattled off some more Huttese, then had a fit of laughter.

"She also says it was really fun to see your reaction," added J-3DI.

"Well, glad my *utter terror* could be entertaining for you," said Rieve. "What are you doing down here, Balada?"

She spoke directly to Rieve, and J-3DI provided the translation. Balada had seen what was going down in her arena from her ship, and she'd sent some of her personal guards to help evacuate the crowd. Then she decided she wasn't going to let the Hunters save the arena by themselves.

"I brought you to Vespaara," said Balada through J-3DI. "You're my responsibility, and I won't abandon you."

Rieve was thankful to hear that. In as brief a manner as possible, she explained what had happened between her and Rothwell, including Rothwell's plan to sabotage the arena to start a new fighting competition.

Balada was quiet for a moment. Then, through J-3DI, she said: "I will crush *anyone* who thinks they can take what I have built."

"Okay, I'm staying here," said Rieve. "I want to be able to see every part of the arena and communicate to the others where Rothwell's goons are. And maybe spot Rothwell himself, though I suspect he isn't out there."

"I have returned power to the arena," said J-3DI, "so it should be easier to see now."

"Beautiful," said Rieve. She rushed over to the screens in the center of the backstage area, then looked at each of the surveillance feeds.

"I don't see Rothwell," she said, defeated. "Just his fighters."

"I can search the underbelly of the arena," said J-3DI. "I have the complete blueprints and layout of this place in my memory."

"Oh, Jay-Three, that would help so much," she said. "Thank you."

He nodded. "May the Force be with you."

Finally! she thought.

"May the Force be with you, too," she returned.

Balada said something and then slithered toward J-3DI.

"You're coming with me?" he said.

Balada laughed, then said something that made J-3DI stand up straighter.

"Well, Balada the Hutt, I would be grateful to have a warrior of your stature at my side."

With that, the two exited backstage, and Rieve got to work.

"Come in, Hunters, come in!" said Rieve. "This is Rieve at mission control, ready to—"

"Rieve, it's so good to hear your voice!" said Zaina. "What should we do?"

Rieve was surprised at how easy it was for her to fall into this role. She had struggled for so long with what it meant to be part of a team, and now it suddenly made sense.

She didn't always have to fight.

She was used to the physical contact, but this? This was what Dragus had been trying to get her to understand. You could play multiple roles. You could help others if you just saw things differently.

Rieve called out each and every one of Rothwell's goons in the arena, directing the Hunters to their locations. Some of them were hiding in the treetops in the Ewok Village, trying to tear the arena apart, or they were sticking detonators on the pylons in the Huttball battlefield. But none of them could hide from Rieve, who soon learned how to maneuver the remote cameras from the control board. She watched with joy as Rothwell's goons were cut down, knocked out, or in the case of an unfortunate Dyplotid, literally tossed into the stands by a no-longer-unconscious Tuya, who cheered as she did so.

"Heads up!" called out Zaina. "Rieve, are you seeing this? Looks like someone's trying to get in the arena. Is that Rothwell?"

Rieve darted over to another one of the feeds. "I see *someone*," she said. "Coming down from the top of the stands near the Ewok Village."

"I have my heavy repeater trained on them," said Sentinel. "Did they *climb* into the arena? How did they get up there?"

The figure was wearing some sort of combat gear.

"Ready to fire on your call," said Sentinel.

Rieve squinted at the monitor.

No.

Could that be . . . ?

"Hold your fire!" she screamed. "That's not Rothwell!"

A smile spread across her face.

"That's Dragus!"

R *IEVE STARED IN SHOCK* at the now-shirtless Dragus as he yelled and slammed together the massive armored gauntlets on his hands. He stepped up to the edge of the stands with his matching armored boots and leapt into the arena. Those same boots helped him land smoothly, and he rose, spreading his arms wide so Rieve (and all Rothwell's goons) could see the thick metallic band around the waist of his tight red pants.

He looked *terrifying*.

Dragus let out another primal yell. "Time for you to meet the mighty power of Durasteel!"

Cries and whoops of victory lit up the comms, and even

Rieve couldn't hold back. "Yes!" she yelled. "Get 'em, Durasteel!"

Which was exactly what he did, aided by Sentinel and Zaina. Over in the Tatooine Outpost, Grozz and Dizzy were making quick work of some human fighters, each of them clad in the brown combat gear Rieve remembered from the alley on Corellia. She ran to a different screen to observe Utooni and Imara Vex in the Gauntlet battlefield, and that's when she saw *him*, walking out into the center of the Aftermath battle-field set on Hoth.

"I have eyes on Rothwell!" said Rieve. "Who can get to Aftermath quickest?"

"Smart money is on me!" said Imara Vex, and Rieve watched as she sprinted from one end of the Ewok Village to the other, then disappeared into the team entrance tunnel.

Rieve's skin prickled. Okay, she'd found Rothwell. What was he planning? His invasion of the arena had already gotten away from him, and it was only a matter of time before the Hunters took care of his goons. They could repair all the damaged parts of the arena, too.

Why was he being so *obvious*?

"I'm almost to Aftermath," said Dragus. "Is Rothwell still there?"

Rieve looked back to the screen with Rothwell on it, and she watched as Imara Vex *and* Dragus appeared on opposite sides of the battlefield.

Rothwell was standing motionless in the center.

An odd sensation passed through Rieve, sending goosebumps over her skin. Something was wrong.

Was this her paranoia?

Was it the Force?

"Please be careful," said Rieve. "I don't have a good feeling about this."

Dragus and Imara Vex approached Rothwell carefully.

"Rieve, can you hear me?"

J-3DI. Wasn't he with Balada the Hutt?

"Yes, but I'm kind of busy at the moment," she said.

"Rieve, it's about Rothwell."

She froze.

And now that feeling crept up her back, and she spun around.

"Rieve!" yelled Dragus. "Rieve! Come in! You need to get out of there!"

"Rieve, Balada and I found a container hidden beneath backstage," said J-3DI. "It is full of holographic matrices."

"Rieve!" Dragus sounded out of breath, like he was running. "Rieve, Rothwell isn't here! It was one of his goons in disguise. It's a hologram disguise matrix!"

"I know," she said quietly. "Because he's here."

Rothwell stood across from Rieve in a much smaller cloak that fit tight across his shoulders. A smile twisted up his face. "It was not as hard to get you alone as I expected," he said. "You are *truly* the most easily manipulated person I've ever met, Rieve."

"Your plan is pointless," she said, her voice shaking. She reached behind her and put her hand on the hilt of her lightsaber, which she'd set on the control board. "We've taken out your men. Balada's arena will need some repairs, but you *failed*."

"I don't care about that anymore," he said. "I just want to make you suffer."

"You already have, Rothwell," she said, and her anger swirled in her chest. "You tried to turn my friends against me. You tried to hurt me in the arena. You left me for dead. So take what you have and get lost."

"No." He said it with so much certainty that it sent a chill through Rieve.

"You can't hurt me," said Rieve.

"Watch me," said Rothwell, and then she saw the blaster, and it was too late.

Rothwell fired.

32

**T ALL HAPPENED SO QUICKLY.**

It all happened so *slowly*.

Rieve cried out as Rothwell fired, and she reacted.

She felt energy surge in her, just like what had happened in the alley, but this time, she focused it all on Rothwell. She swung her lightsaber around and activated it, blocking the first blaster shot.

But Rothwell kept firing.

It was an instant.

It seemed to last forever.

She willed her body to the right, wishing she could just disappear so Rothwell's blaster fire wouldn't kill her.

And to her great shock, her body *moved*. She flew to the side, so fast that the only thing that could stop her was one of the prep pods. She slammed into it and dropped to the ground, her lightsaber flying away from her. Pain flared up her left arm.

Had Rothwell done that? A new fear grew in her: was he a Force user, too?

"Rieve! Rieve, come in! Where are you? Are you okay?"

She didn't know who was yelling at her through the comms. It didn't matter right then. She hoisted herself up as quickly as she could, and Rothwell—very much *not* a hologram— looked *impressed*.

"I admit I did not expect that," he said, his free hand on his chest and a smile spreading from ear to ear. "It's not going to help you, though."

She groaned loudly as she felt a new ache on her side. She really wished she had some of that magical med tape Balada had the Hunters wear in the arena.

Rothwell still had his blaster trained on Rieve, but he approached her slowly. "You really don't know what you're doing," he said, shaking his head. "You have all this power, Rieve, and yet all you leave in your wake is *destruction*."

"Power?"

Oh.

She had somehow flung *herself* across the room in some sort of . . . what? Force-assisted burst of speed? Was that even a thing?

Rothwell must have seen Rieve's epiphany on her face. "Oh, catch up, Rieve," he said. "I knew what you were capable of years ago when you blasted the sanity out of my people. It's not my fault you've wasted it being a meaningless *nothing* here on Vespaara. I'm only here to make you pay the price."

"It's over," said Rieve, hoping that the other Hunters were listening to her over the comms. "We've taken care of your goons, and your plan didn't work."

"Is this where you give me some big heroic speech?" said Rothwell. "Because *that* doesn't suit you, Rieve. You're not a hero."

He was closer now.

"You're a coward. You ran from me and the damage you caused all those years ago, and when it comes down to it, you'll run again. You will save your own hide before you ever help out any of these people."

"You make it sound like I purposefully sought you and your men out," said Rieve. "You keep trying to manipulate me into thinking what happened in that alley was *evil.*"

"You destroyed my family," said Rothwell calmly. "How is that not evil?"

"Your choices got you there," she said. "I know that now. I was doing my job, and your couriers and guards didn't care about that. I was blaming myself for that day long before you showed up here on Vespaara, Rothwell. And trust me, hating myself was a lot easier than accepting that I was a confused, scared *teenager!*"

She screamed that last part, so loudly that Rothwell actually flinched.

"I had to defend myself against grown men trying to hurt me," she added. "How does that make *me* the villain?"

"How *moral,*" he said, striding forward once more, his

blaster still trained on Rieve. "But you're the one in the wrong here."

She spotted it then, just under a table behind Rothwell.

Her lightsaber.

Rieve was defenseless up against the prep pod, but . . . she'd done it once before. Could she do it again?

She closed her eyes for a brief moment.

How? How had she been able to move so quickly before?

She opened her eyes.

Rothwell held his blaster pistol a meter from her face.

"Say goodbye, Rieve," he said.

He pulled the trigger.

She willed herself to move.

The room blurred around her as she dashed forward, past Rothwell, and this time she didn't slam into anything. She controlled her stop and reached out for her lightsaber. When her hand came in contact with the hilt, she spun about and brought it in front of her, the red blade hissing to life.

"Stay *still*!" Rothwell screamed. "Why can't you just stay in one place and die?"

He let loose a barrage of blaster fire, and Rieve swung her lightsaber to deflect it. She rolled, flipped a table sideways, and hid behind it. Rothwell kept firing, screaming as he did so.

And then Rieve made her move.

As soon as Rothwell paused, she darted up from behind the table and focused all her energy and willpower on his blaster. She flung her lightsaber toward him, and it spun in the air until the blade sliced through the blaster. Rothwell cried out in shock, and she willed the lightsaber to return to her.

It spun back, and the hilt landed perfectly in her hand.

She had never felt this kind of elation before. Maybe, in some small way, Rothwell was right: Rieve really didn't know how much power she had. She'd thrown her lightsaber in the arena before but *never* with such precision.

"Rieve!"

To her right, Dragus appeared, his blaster raised. "Hands up, Rothwell!" he called out.

Rieve smiled.

It was over.

Rothwell backed toward one of the tunnels that led to the battlefields. "No, I don't think so," he said.

He pulled something out of the folds of his cloak and held it up in front of him.

"Oh, *great*," said Dragus, who was closest to it.

Rieve knew what it was; she'd delivered a few of them during her days in Coronet City.

A thermal detonator.

Rieve *hated* thermal detonators. To her, such explosives were a coward's weapon. So it didn't surprise her that Rothwell wielded one.

"Unless you let me leave," he said, "I drop this. You have maybe ten seconds to get out of here before this entire area is destroyed."

"You lost," said Dragus. "Face it, Rothwell. Rieve got you. There's nowhere for you to go."

As if on cue, Rieve's teammates—Sentinel, Zaina, Imara Vex, Utooni, Grozz, and Dizzy—poured out of one of the tunnels that led to the battlefields.

And from the stairwell that led to the central core . . .

J-3DI.

"You're outnumbered," said Rieve. "Nine to one. Just give up."

"No," said Rothwell. "I'm not outnumbered with a detonator."

"He is holding a Class-A thermal detonator," said J-3DI, "most favored by stormtrooper grenadiers and other parts of the Galactic Empire's military."

"Well aware of that!" said Sentinel. "I left the Empire for a million reasons, and not having to see one of those ever again is one of them!"

"It has a blast radius up to twenty meters and an arming phase from six to eighteen seconds."

"Thanks, Jay-Three," said Dragus sarcastically. "Glad you're narrating this for us."

"My pleasure!" the droid said happily.

Rieve was tired. Tired of waiting for Rothwell to make a move, tired of doubting herself, tired of this man *making* her doubt herself. Her anger returned then, and she stepped forward.

"Rieve," said Rothwell, pointing the detonator in her direction. "Don't think about it. If I even *sense* you using your silly mystical powers on me, I'll activate it."

"I know," she said, and she took another step forward. "I believe you."

"Just let him go," said Sentinel. "It's not worth it."

"Things can be rebuilt," added Dragus, who stood motionless near Rothwell.

Way too near Rothwell for Rieve's comfort.

"Just give it up, Rothwell," she said. "Put the detonator on the floor, and we won't hurt you."

"I can't promise that," said Sentinel. "I didn't get to punch enough people today."

Rieve took another step forward.

"Stop," said Rothwell, holding the detonator closer to Dragus.

"Allow me," said J-3DI. "I can move swiftly and take the detonator to a less populated area for it to explode."

Rieve turned and glared at him. "No!" she said. "Absolutely not. It'll destroy you."

He was quiet for a moment. "That is all right with me. Sprocket can always build another version of me."

"I'm faster," said Dizzy. "Me and my droideka . . . I bet I could get it deep into one of the tunnels and then chuck it away from me."

"I've got a better throwing arm," said Zaina. "I should be the one to take Rothwell down."

"We could always do it *together*," said Dragus, desperation in his voice. "There *are* nine of us, after all."

The Hunters and Dragus continued to argue over who could best dispose of the thermal detonator Rothwell held. Each of them was willing to put themselves at great risk to protect this arena. To protect *her*. Even though none of this would have happened if she hadn't come here in the first place.

Rieve knew that *she* had to be the one to clean up this mess.

"All of you, shut *up*!" she bellowed.

Silence fell. Even Rothwell looked at Rieve with anticipation.

"This has always been my problem," she said. "Let *me* take care of it."

Before any of them could protest, Rothwell groaned dramatically. "Are you all going to stand here and debate which one of you is the best hero? I'm going to die of boredom just *listening* to you."

He raised the detonator.

"I really don't care what happens to any of you."

He pressed the arming button.

"Good luck, Rieve," he said. "You're gonna need it."

Then, as he twisted away, heading straight for an exit tunnel, the armed detonator plummeted to the floor and rolled over to Dragus's feet.

RIEVE MOVED.

The Force flowed through her as she dashed straight to the detonator, which beeped rapidly on the floor. She could see the others all heading in the same direction, each of them convinced they could stop the inevitable.

No one could.

But as Rieve reached the detonator, as she snatched it from the ground at Dragus's feet, the voice came to her suddenly.

Not in the usual tone.

Not with the same dire anger that had always been there.

Something *new*.

You can save them all.

The detonator let her know it was still armed:

Beep–beep–beep–beep–beep.

Could she?

She breathed in deep.

Rieve *pushed*.

It was gentle, nothing like what she'd done to Dragus the last time she was in this room. She channeled the Force through her body, and then she shoved outward.

All of them—the Hunters and Dragus—slid away from her.

Time slowed to a drip, and she heard Dragus yell, "Rieve, what are you doing?"

She ignored him.

Her fellow Hunters skidded to a stop at the walls of the room.

You can save them all.

Beep–beep–beep–beep–beep.

Rothwell, who had not quite made it to the exit and had been thrown to the floor by the Force, stood up and tried to move, but Rieve held him in place.

Beep–beep–beep–beep–beep.

Someone called out her name.

She ignored it.

Beep-beep-beep-beep-beep.

The truth was that she didn't really know what she was doing. Instinct was guiding her, and it told her that this was possible.

So she set the detonator on the floor in front of her.

Beep-beep-beep-beep-beep.

And she waited for it to explode.

34

RIEVE FOCUSED ALL HER WILLPOWER on this one object.

She felt it build up and swirl inside of her like before, but this time there was a key difference:

She did not let that voice control her.

She controlled *it*.

Her anger. Her rage. Her disappointment.

They were a part of her. They might always be. But instead of directing them at herself, instead of believing that no one cared for her, that she'd always be alone, she channeled those emotions *outward*. It was like she was onstage again, using music to express what she felt deep inside.

All it took was concentration and willpower.

No. Not just that. There was one more thing.

Rieve *had* to believe in herself.

She repeated what the new voice had told her, only this time, she said it aloud.

"I can save them all."

Beep-beep-beep-beep.

Rieve sent *all* her energy into the thermal detonator, sweat pouring down her temples as she did so. She no longer held the others back with the Force, but she hoped they understood not to come any closer. The sensation passed down her arms, into the device, and she imagined all that power in her own hands.

She cried out.

And the detonator *exploded*.

There was a vicious brightness, but Rieve clung to it, held on to the blast by using a Force pull. She held a swirling mass of light and fire in front of her.

I can save them all.

She groaned as the heat and power of the explosion began

to crawl up her arms and into her body. Her costume singed at the edges, and smoke rose into the air.

"Rieve!" Dragus cried out.

She held on to that massive, swirling, chaotic energy in front of her, but she was shaking, violently so, because something of that magnitude could not be controlled for very long. It felt like she held her hands around the neck of a snarling nexu as it snapped at her face.

Rieve had to do something with it.

The skin on her hands blistered, and she screamed in pain. Perhaps this was enough, and she had weakened the blast. That was all she needed to do. If she could take on some of that power, she could save them all.

But she also wasn't sure she could hold on to it much longer.

"Down!" she screamed.

And then Rieve let go.

The blast catapulted Rieve backward until she hit a prep pod behind her, then dropped to the ground. She saw a terrible brightness in her vision as she struggled for air on the floor, and she worried that she'd not done enough, that the blast had taken out her friends.

Her family.

Rieve heard yelling and she tried to stand, but her legs wobbled. She glanced at her hands, red from the heat of the explosion, and saw that the sleeves of her arena costume had completely burned away.

"Rieve! Rieve!"

Someone was in her field of vision, but she couldn't focus.

"Rieve, can you hear me?"

She blinked.

The blue light of J-3DI's left eye was incredibly close to her face.

"Jay-Three!" she cried.

She wanted to hug the droid, but her hands throbbed and stung.

She was *alive*.

J-3DI moved out of the way, and the first thing Rieve saw was the smoking, scorched remains of the monitor system and the control board. J-3DI helped her up as she swayed with dizziness, and she saw the other Hunters coming over to her. Uninjured.

"What?" she muttered. "Is everyone okay?"

Zaina was next at Rieve's side. "Rieve, what *was* that?" she asked. "You just—It was like—I don't really know what to say."

There was a crash behind Zaina, and a chunk of the ceiling rolled off the smoldering control board.

"How bad is the damage?" Rieve asked.

"Nowhere near as bad as it should be," said Sentinel. "That was . . . incredible. I've never seen anything like it."

"Let go of me!" she heard Rothwell say.

Sentinel stepped out of the way as Dragus hobbled over, holding Rothwell firmly by the arm. Rothwell had his other hand up to his forehead. He was bleeding.

Rieve couldn't help it. Even though she wasn't exactly in the best state herself, she smiled.

"You lost, Rothwell," she said, stepping up to him. "I still have the arena *and* my family."

Her family. That was what they were, weren't they? How

many times had they volunteered to help train her? Or looked past her mistakes and believed that she would get better? Or done their best to help her feel like she belonged?

Dragus grinned. "Nice job doing . . . whatever it was you just did."

"Thanks," she said.

"Maybe that could be like . . ." Dragus paused. "I don't know. Your signature move?"

"Please stop working," said Imara Vex. "We're not on the job right now."

It *was* a good idea, though. Rieve finally let relief wash over her as her teammates congratulated and thanked her.

She'd done it.

She'd saved them all.

 **HE OTHERS HELPED RIEVE OUT OF** the arena, since she was still weak from what she'd done backstage. Once she was outside, Dragus hailed some of the medic team for immediate help. But Rieve was most surprised by the presence of Balada the Hutt. She slid over to Rieve, one of her short arms extended.

"Jupa uba," she said.

Rieve raised an eyebrow and looked to Dragus.

"Even if you spoke Huttese, I would be surprised if you knew that one," he said. "She said *thank you.*"

Rieve looked back at her, and she saw warmth in Balada's eyes. "Thank you for letting me be here," said Rieve. "If you'll still have me."

Balada gave a belly laugh as she slithered away.

"I'm going with her and taking this one with me," said Dragus, tugging on a defeated Rothwell. "We'll head up to Balada's ship and then turn him and his goons over to the authorities."

Rieve stepped up to Rothwell, whose face drooped. "You smuggled for the Empire," she said. "I didn't ruin your life. *They* did. You need to accept that."

Rothwell had nothing to say to that. After all his performances, after all that manipulation, he was silent. What could he say? She had persevered despite his abuse, despite the story about her that he'd invented in his own mind.

Dragus dragged him off, and Rieve hoped that she would never see Rothwell again.

Rieve turned around and approached the large circular hole in the middle of the Outpost battlefield. "Not bad," she said.

J-3DI came up to Rieve. "The damage below is significant," he said. "But you greatly reduced the impact of the detonator's blast and saved most of backstage."

"Well, that's a relief," she said.

He hesitated. "That was an impressive display of the Force," he continued. "I am sad to say I only have bits and pieces of lore to possibly explain it. But perhaps you could do it again, and we could measure it."

"Thank . . . you?" said Rieve. "I think it has to be a limited thing, though. I'm exhausted, Jay-Three."

"Understood," he said. "I have much to attend to now. But I just want to say: it is clear I have a lot to learn from you, Master."

And then he walked back into the arena.

"So do you believe us now?" said Zaina, stepping forward. "We're not giving up on you, Rieve."

Rieve offered up a quick smile. "I'm adjusting," she said. "I had no family back on Corellia. This is all very new to me."

"Plus, no one gets to hurt you," said Imara Vex. "No one but *me*, that is."

The group laughed, and the voice spoke in her mind.

You're safe.

It was the first time she'd ever felt safe.

She was adjusting to that, too.

The medics arrived, and she was whisked away for treatment. The last thing she saw before they took her was the other Hunters waving at her.

Her family.

**IEVE BREATHED IN.**

Breathed out.

You can do this, the voice said.

She stood at the edge of the new battlefield, which had been constructed at the same time as the repairs to fix what the detonator had done backstage. Balada was considering making it another Huttball battlefield, but for now it was to host a brand-new type of match.

Things were changing so quickly in Rieve's life. Sentinel had visited her at home, and she'd actually let him inside to see her place. That was followed not long after by Imara Vex, Zaina, and Grozz bursting in, dragging Rieve and Sentinel out for a night at the Oasis Cantina. That was happening a lot: her fellow Hunters *actually* wanted to get to know her.

It was nice.

Rothwell had been shipped off-planet the day before, stuck on a transport with his fighters that was heading to a New Republic colony. Someone had sent an anonymous message to the New Republic authorities that would ensure that Rothwell wouldn't be seen around Vespaara for a long, long time.

So there she was, waiting for the match to begin. She stood with the three other Hunters on her team for the day's match: J-3DI. Imara Vex. Grozz.

She wasn't competing against the other four Hunters that night, though.

The chime-bell went off. They rushed onto the battlefield.

A large metal gate creaked open on the opposite end.

And an enormous, hideous creature strode into the arena, its jaws slick with saliva, its claws sharp and terrible.

"That is a rancor," said J-3DI to the others over comms. "Native to Dathomir in the Quelli sector and—"

"And clearly it's going to eat us," said Imara Vex. "What do you say we make a meal of it first?"

"Lead the way, Rieve," said J-3DI.

Rieve smiled.

She liked the sound of that.

So she charged that horrific beast, her teammates close behind her, and when it swiped at Rieve, she slid between its legs. It roared in frustration, and she took her chance to leap onto its back.

Grozz hollered something victorious.

There, on the back of a dangerous, bloodthirsty creature, with her Hunter friends ready for her next command, Rieve finally felt like she was exactly where she needed to be.

ACKNOWLEDGMENTS

MY ETERNAL THANKS to my agent, DongWon Song, for their support and helping make my dream come true.

Thank you to my *Star Wars* author family, especially Zoraida Córdova, for your guidance and support.

There were many, *many* people involved in the creation of this book, which was the first like it that I'd ever done. First, I must thank the folks at Disney Lucasfilm Press. My brilliant editor, Jennifer Heddle, guided me through this story and helped me find the heart of it. Thank you to Andie Tong for the illustrations; you have given this lifelong *Star Wars* fan a gift. Thank you to Jason Wojtowicz, Megan Speer, and Lyssa Hurvitz for all your work in making this book a reality.

It was also a life goal of mine to someday get to work with Lucasfilm, and the experience was absolutely everything I ever wanted. Thank you to Kelsey Sharpe, Matt Martin, and Emily Shkoukani of Story Group for your ideas and enthusiasm. High fives to the Lucasfilm Games devision: Matt Fillbrandt, Craig Derrick, Sean Dornan-Fish, Doug Boethling, Hez Chorba, and Ashley Kokawa.

Finally, thanks to the folks at BossAlien for letting me play in your sandbox and create a whole novel out of your game! Particular thanks go to William Wallace, Matthew Hemby, and Ben Brudenell.

May the Force be with you all,
Mark

MARK OSHIRO is the award-winning author of the young adult novels *Anger Is a Gift* and *Each of Us a Desert*, as well as their middle grade debut, *The Insiders*. When they are not writing, they are trying to fulfill their lifelong goal: to pet every dog in the world.

ANDIE TONG'S past comic book and illustration experience includes titles such as *The Legend of Shang-Chi, Spectacular Spider-Man UK, Green Lantern: Legacy, The Batman Strikes, Tron: Betrayal, Plants vs. Zombies, Star Wars, Tekken, Street Fighter, The Wheel of Time,* and Stan Lee's Zodiac Legacy book series.

Andie has also illustrated children's books for Harper-Collins for more then ten years and has had the opportunity to work on multiple books with the late Stan Lee.

Malaysian born, Andie migrated to Australia at a young age and then moved to London in 2005. In 2012, he journeyed back to Asia and currently resides in Singapore with his wife and two children.